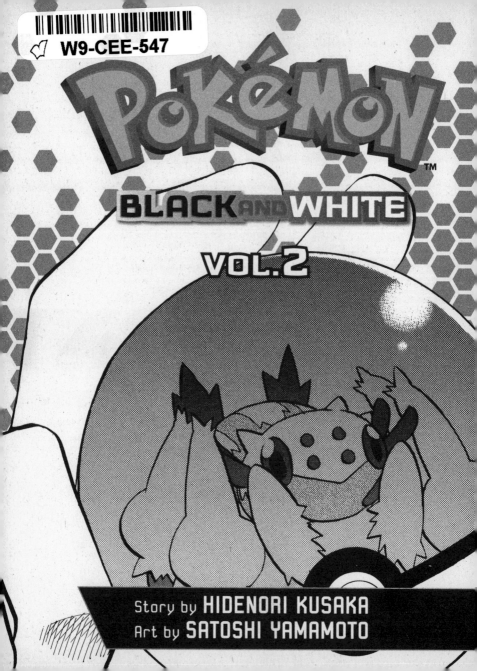

# POKÉMON™

## BLACK AND WHITE

### VOL. 2

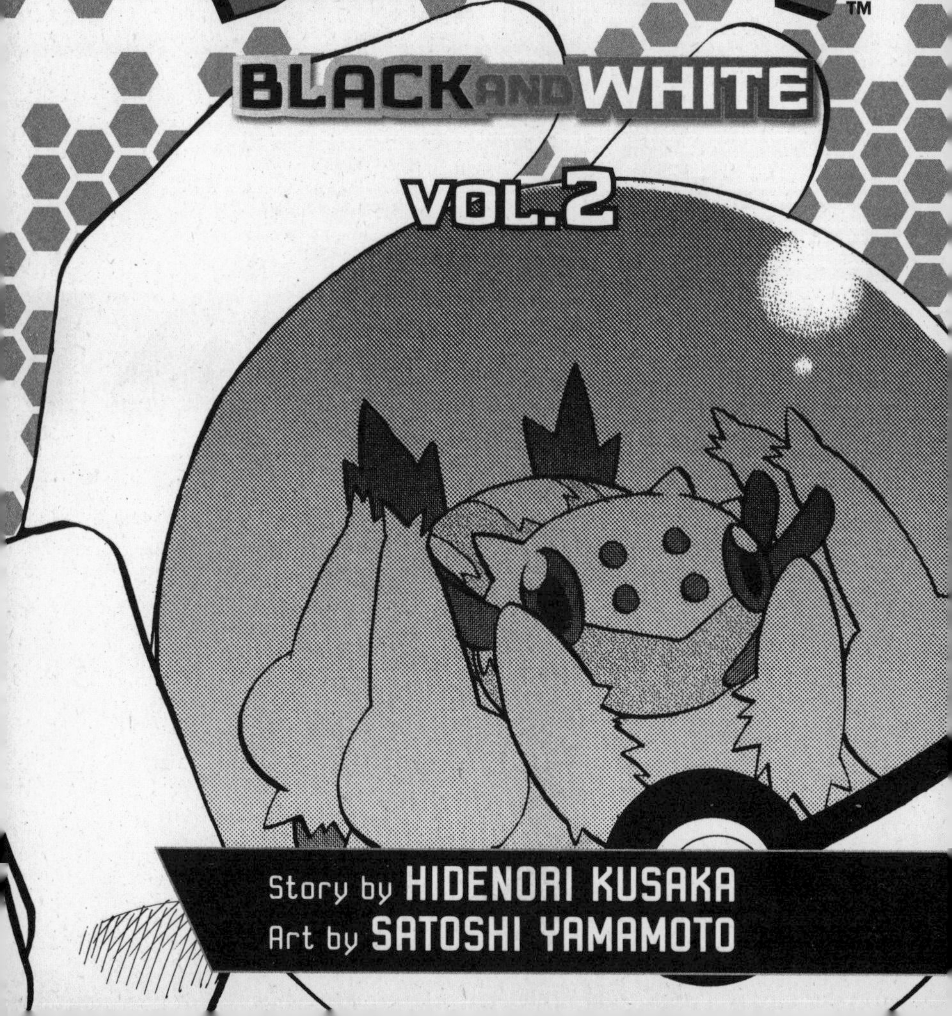

Story by HIDENORI KUSAKA
Art by SATOSHI YAMAMOTO

## Pokémon Black and White
## Volume 2
## VIZ Kids Edition

### Story by HIDENORI KUSAKA
### Art by SATOSHI YAMAMOTO

© 2011 Pokémon.
© 1995–2011 Nintendo/Creatures Inc./GAME FREAK inc.
TM and ® and character names are trademarks of Nintendo.
© 1997 Hidenori KUSAKA and Satoshi YAMAMOTO/Shogakukan
All rights reserved.
Original Japanese edition "POCKET MONSTER SPECIAL"
published by SHOGAKUKAN Inc.

English Adaptation / Annette Roman
Translation / Tetsuichiro Miyaki
Touch-up & Lettering / Susan Daigle-Leach
Design / Fawn Lau
Editor / Annette Roman

Printed in the U.S.A.

Published by VIZ Media, LLC
P.O. Box 77010
San Francisco, CA 94107

10 9 8 7 6 5 4 3 2 1
First printing, July 2011

www.vizkids.com

www.viz.com

# POKÉMON
## BLACK AND WHITE
### VOL.2

# THE STORY THUS FAR!

His entire life Pokémon Trainer Black has dreamed of winning the Pokémon League... Now he has finally embarked on a journey to explore the mysterious Unova region and fill his brand-new Pokédex with data for Professor Juniper.

Black won his first Pokémon Trainer battle ever! What strange new Pokémon—and people—will Black discover on his travels next...?

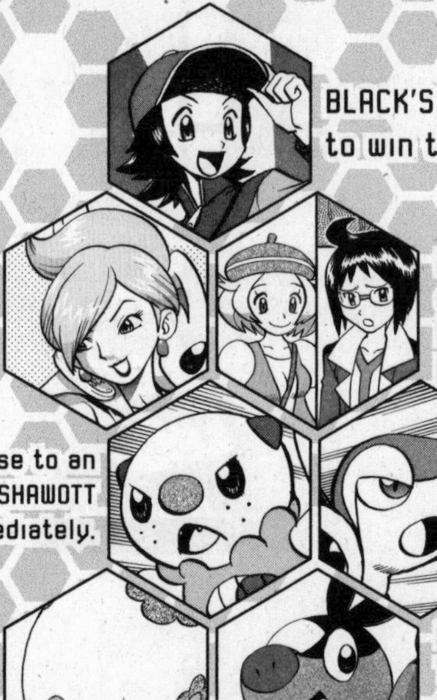

BLACK'S dream is to win the Pokémon League!

PROFESSOR JUNIPER is always eager to learn new things about Pokémon.

Black's friends BIANCA and CHEREN chose Oshawott and Snivy from Professor Juniper's lab. (Actually, Bianca chose Snivy for Cheren!)

In response to an attack, OSHAWOTT retaliates immediately.

Being exposed to lots of sunlight makes SNIVY'S movements swifter.

Black's MUNNA helps him think clearly by temporarily "eating" his dream.

Black's stubborn new Pokémon TEPIG can deftly dodge its foe's attacks while shooting fireballs from its nose.

## Adventure ⑤ Lights, Camera... Action!

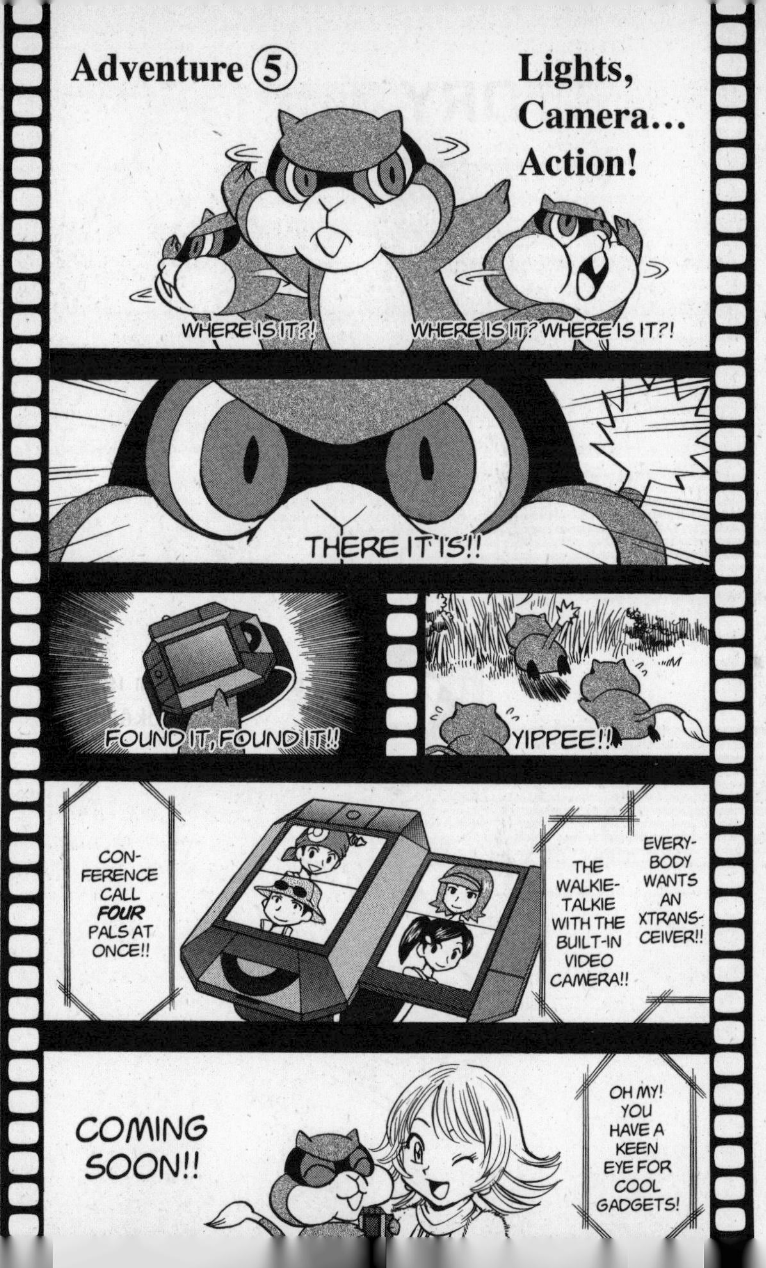
WHERE IS IT?!
WHERE IS IT? WHERE IS IT?!
THERE IT IS!!
FOUND IT, FOUND IT!!
YIPPEE!!
EVERYBODY WANTS AN XTRANSCEIVER!!
THE WALKIE-TALKIE WITH THE BUILT-IN VIDEO CAMERA!!
CONFERENCE CALL FOUR PALS AT ONCE!!
OH MY! YOU HAVE A KEEN EYE FOR COOL GADGETS!
COMING SOON!!

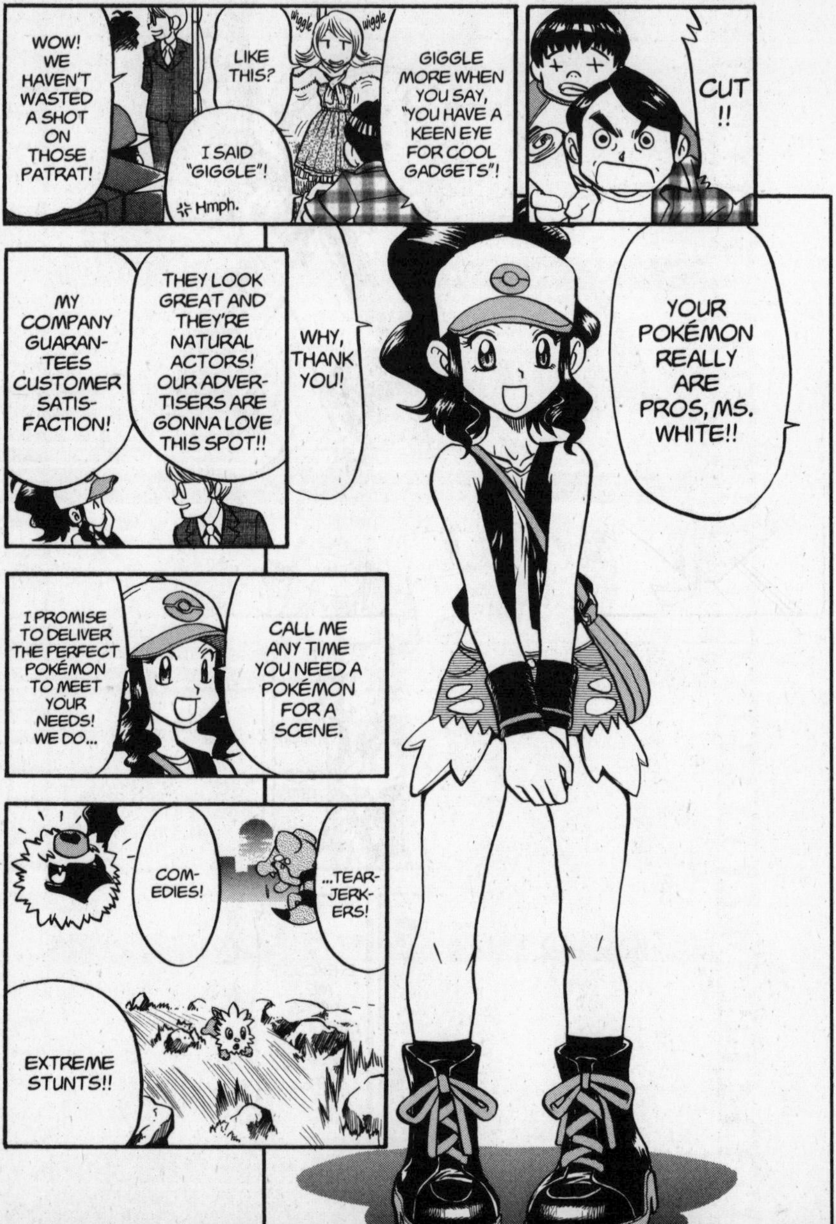
WOW! WE HAVEN'T WASTED A SHOT ON THOSE PATRAT!
LIKE THIS?
wiggle
wiggle
I SAID "GIGGLE"!
Hmph.
GIGGLE MORE WHEN YOU SAY, "YOU HAVE A KEEN EYE FOR COOL GADGETS"!
CUT!!
YOUR POKÉMON REALLY ARE PROS, MS. WHITE!!
WHY, THANK YOU!
THEY LOOK GREAT AND THEY'RE NATURAL ACTORS! OUR ADVERTISERS ARE GONNA LOVE THIS SPOT!!
MY COMPANY GUARANTEES CUSTOMER SATISFACTION!
CALL ME ANY TIME YOU NEED A POKÉMON FOR A SCENE.
I PROMISE TO DELIVER THE PERFECT POKÉMON TO MEET YOUR NEEDS! WE DO...
...TEARJERKERS!
COMEDIES!
EXTREME STUNTS!!

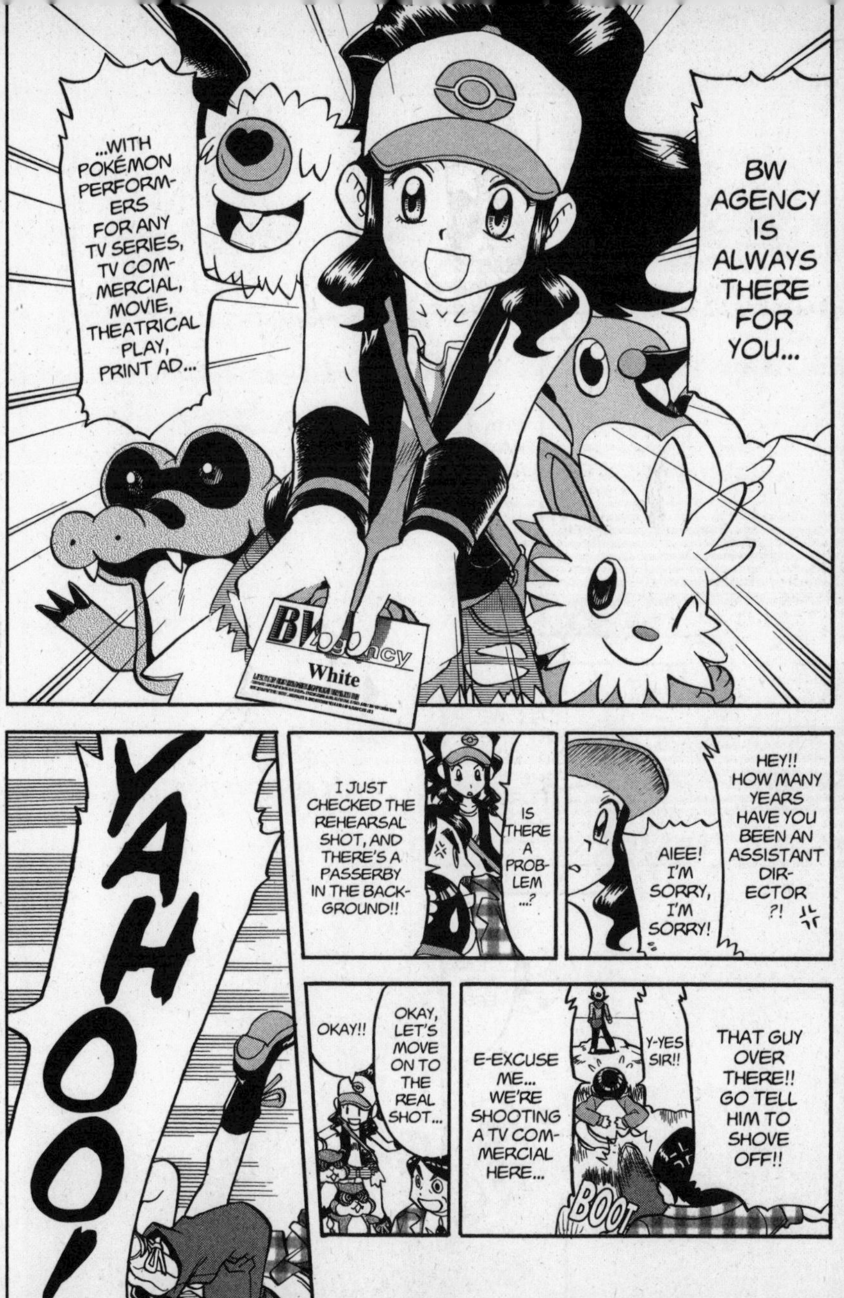
BW AGENCY IS ALWAYS THERE FOR YOU...
...WITH POKÉMON PERFORMERS FOR ANY TV SERIES, TV COMMERCIAL, MOVIE, THEATRICAL PLAY, PRINT AD...
BW Agency
White
HEY!! HOW MANY YEARS HAVE YOU BEEN AN ASSISTANT DIRECTOR?!
AIEE! I'M SORRY, I'M SORRY!
IS THERE A PROBLEM...?
I JUST CHECKED THE REHEARSAL SHOT, AND THERE'S A PASSERBY IN THE BACKGROUND!!
THAT GUY OVER THERE!! GO TELL HIM TO SHOVE OFF!!
Y-YES SIR!!
BOOT
E-EXCUSE ME... WE'RE SHOOTING A TV COMMERCIAL HERE...
OKAY, LET'S MOVE ON TO THE REAL SHOT...
OKAY!!
YAHOO!

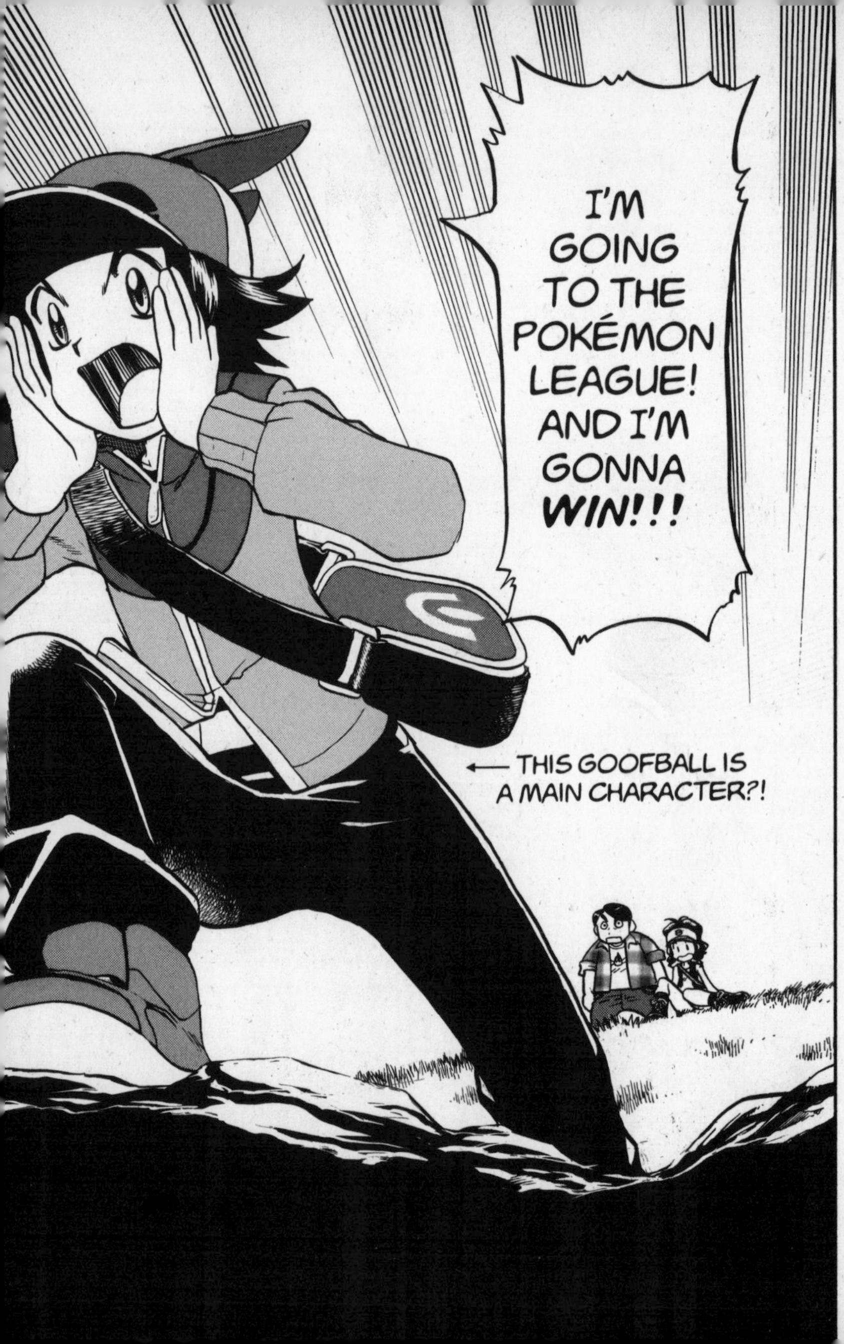
I'M GOING TO THE POKÉMON LEAGUE! AND I'M GONNA WIN!!!
← THIS GOOFBALL IS A MAIN CHARACTER?!

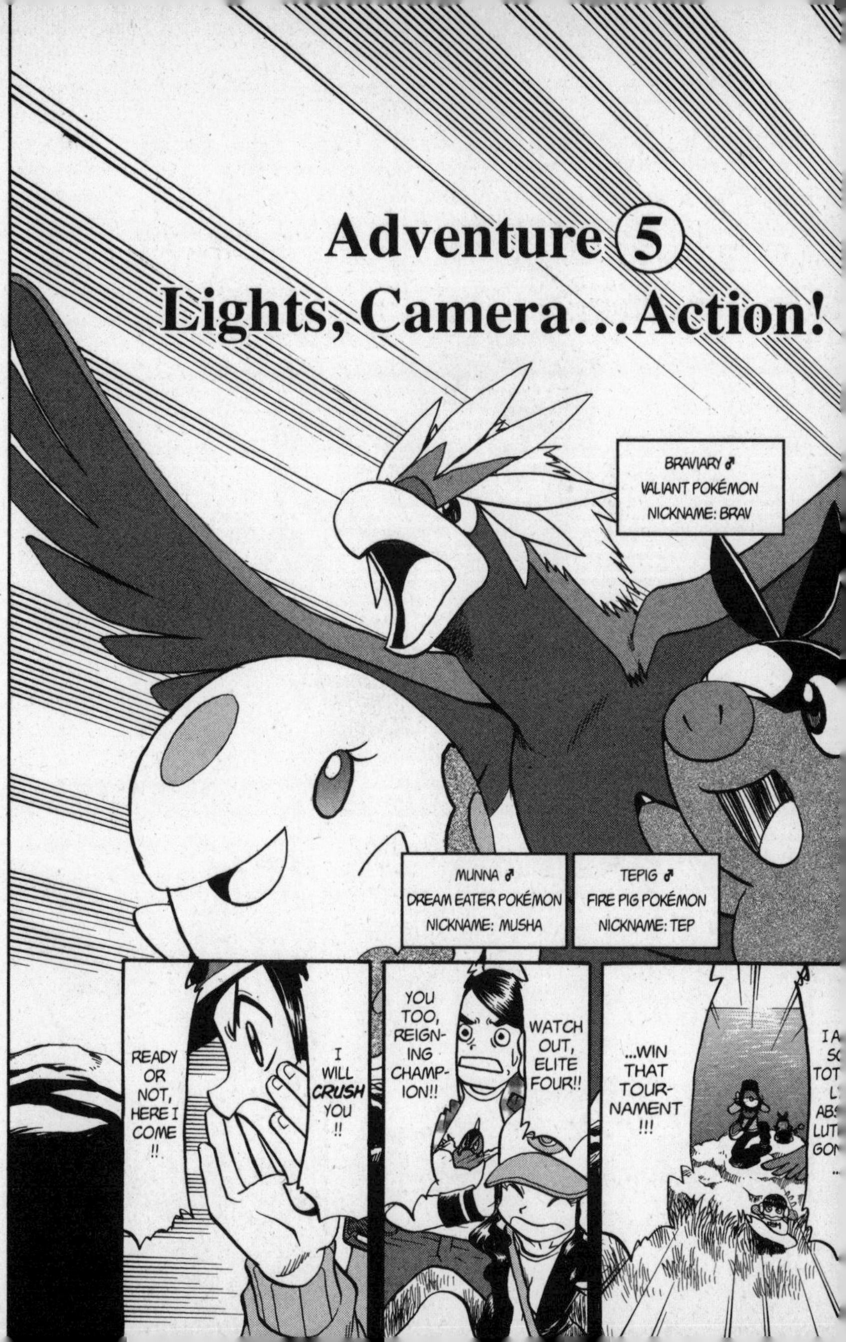

Adventure 5
Lights, Camera...Action!
BRAVIARY ♂
VALIANT POKÉMON
NICKNAME: BRAV
MUNNA ♂
DREAM EATER POKÉMON
NICKNAME: MUSHA
TEPIG ♂
FIRE PIG POKÉMON
NICKNAME: TEP
READY OR NOT, HERE I COME !!
I WILL CRUSH YOU !!
YOU TOO, REIGNING CHAMPION!!
WATCH OUT, ELITE FOUR!!
...WIN THAT TOURNAMENT !!!

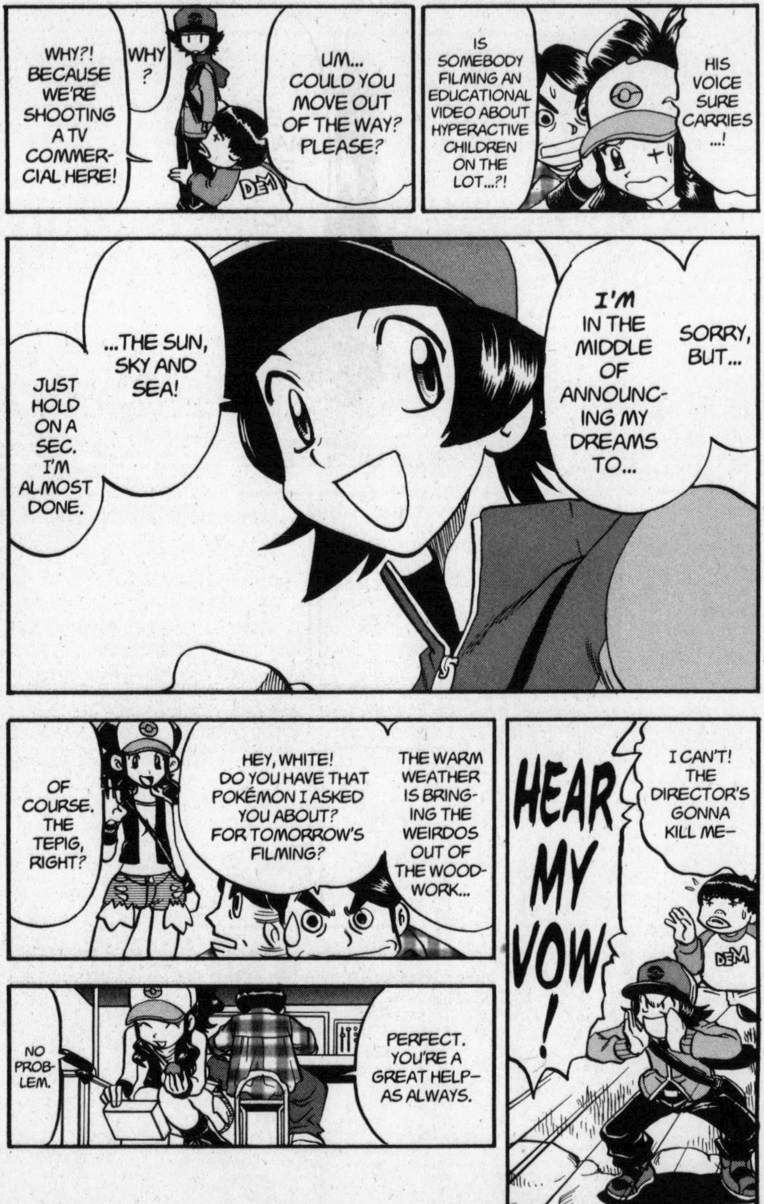
UM... COULD YOU MOVE OUT OF THE WAY? PLEASE?
WHY?
WHY?! BECAUSE WE'RE SHOOTING A TV COMMERCIAL HERE!
DEM
IS SOMEBODY FILMING AN EDUCATIONAL VIDEO ABOUT HYPERACTIVE CHILDREN ON THE LOT...?!
HIS VOICE SURE CARRIES...!
SORRY, BUT...
I'M IN THE MIDDLE OF ANNOUNCING MY DREAMS TO...
...THE SUN, SKY AND SEA!
JUST HOLD ON A SEC. I'M ALMOST DONE.
I CAN'T! THE DIRECTOR'S GONNA KILL ME—
HEAR MY VOW!
DEM
THE WARM WEATHER IS BRINGING THE WEIRDOS OUT OF THE WOODWORK...
HEY, WHITE! DO YOU HAVE THAT POKÉMON I ASKED YOU ABOUT? FOR TOMORROW'S FILMING?
OF COURSE. THE TEPIG, RIGHT?
PERFECT. YOU'RE A GREAT HELP—AS ALWAYS.
NO PROBLEM.

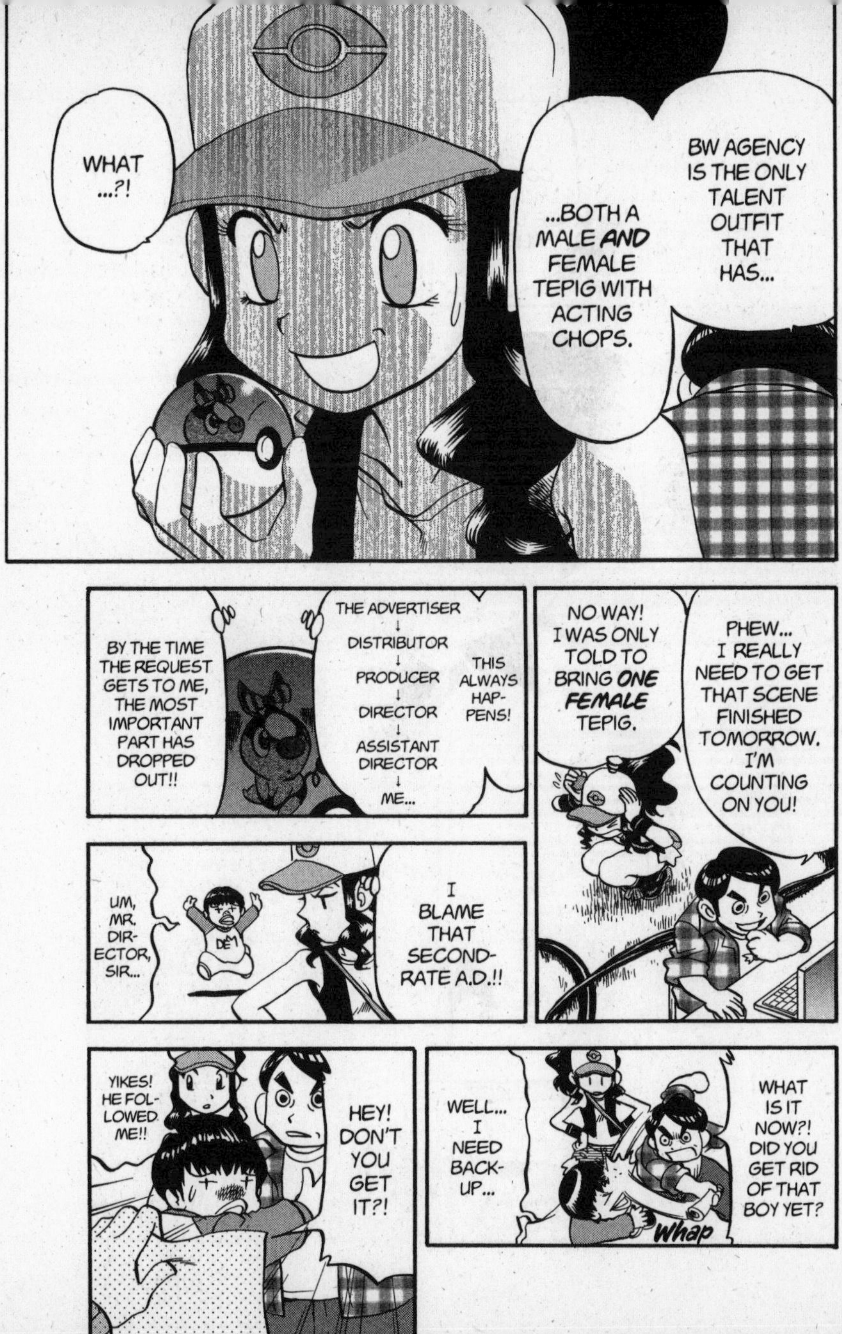
BW AGENCY IS THE ONLY TALENT OUTFIT THAT HAS...
...BOTH A MALE AND FEMALE TEPIG WITH ACTING CHOPS.
WHAT ...?!
PHEW... I REALLY NEED TO GET THAT SCENE FINISHED TOMORROW. I'M COUNTING ON YOU!
NO WAY! I WAS ONLY TOLD TO BRING ONE FEMALE TEPIG.
THE ADVERTISER ↓ DISTRIBUTOR ↓ PRODUCER ↓ DIRECTOR ↓ ASSISTANT DIRECTOR ↓ ME...
THIS ALWAYS HAP-PENS!
BY THE TIME THE REQUEST GETS TO ME, THE MOST IMPORTANT PART HAS DROPPED OUT!!
I BLAME THAT SECOND-RATE A.D.!!
UM, MR. DIR-ECTOR, SIR...
DEM
WHAT IS IT NOW?! DID YOU GET RID OF THAT BOY YET?
WELL... I NEED BACK-UP...
Whap
HEY! DON'T YOU GET IT?!
YIKES! HE FOL-LOWED ME!!

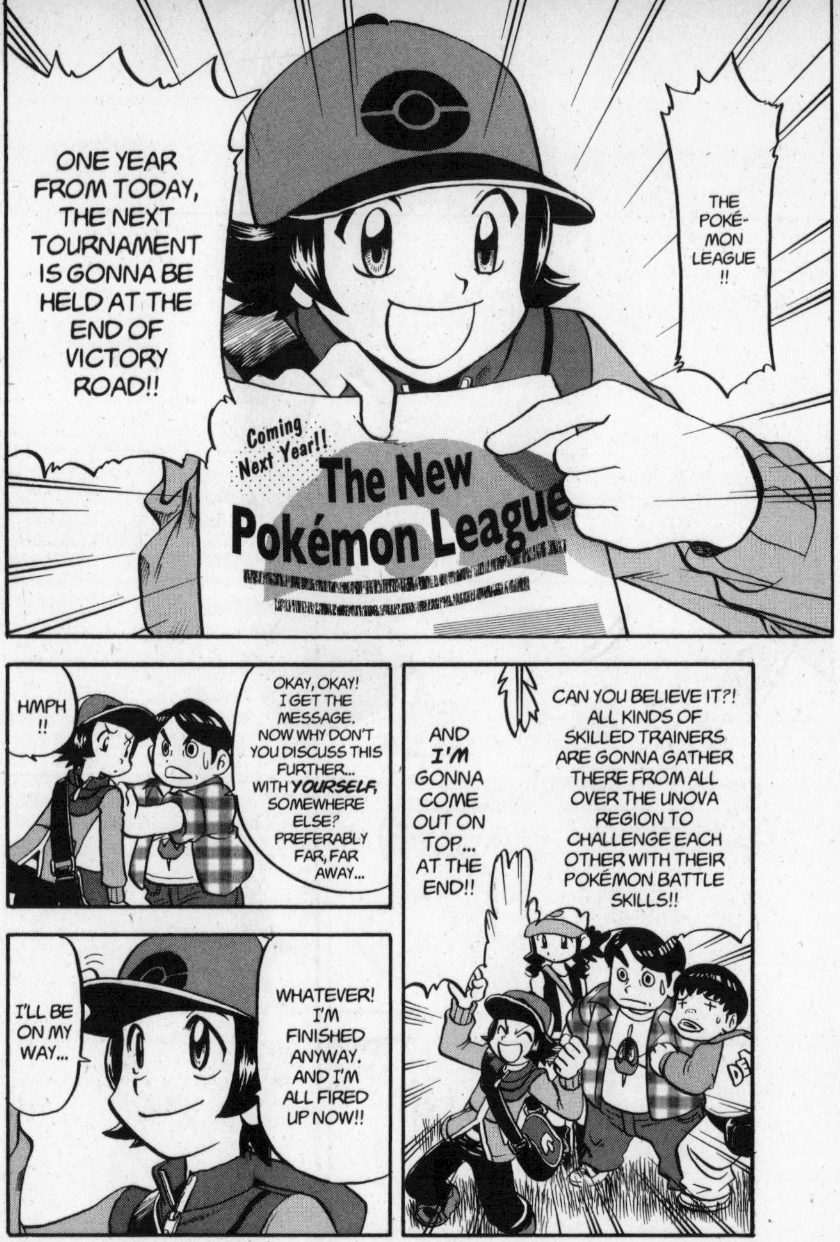
ONE YEAR FROM TODAY, THE NEXT TOURNAMENT IS GONNA BE HELD AT THE END OF VICTORY ROAD!!
THE POKÉMON LEAGUE!!
Coming Next Year!!
The New Pokémon League
HMPH!!
OKAY, OKAY! I GET THE MESSAGE. NOW WHY DON'T YOU DISCUSS THIS FURTHER... WITH YOURSELF, SOMEWHERE ELSE? PREFERABLY FAR, FAR AWAY...
CAN YOU BELIEVE IT?! ALL KINDS OF SKILLED TRAINERS ARE GONNA GATHER THERE FROM ALL OVER THE UNOVA REGION TO CHALLENGE EACH OTHER WITH THEIR POKÉMON BATTLE SKILLS!!
AND I'M GONNA COME OUT ON TOP... AT THE END!!
I'LL BE ON MY WAY...
WHATEVER! I'M FINISHED ANYWAY. AND I'M ALL FIRED UP NOW!!

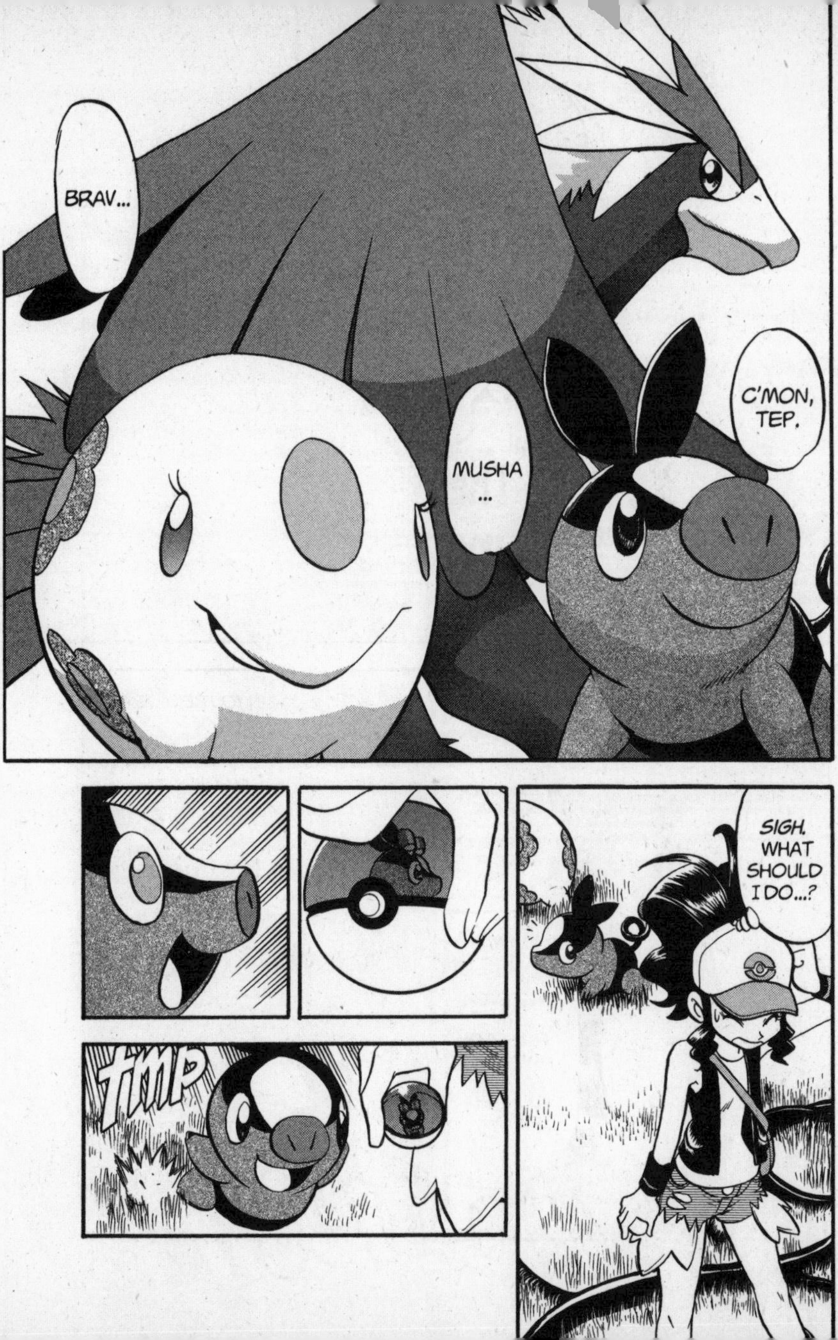
C'MON, TEP.
MUSHA ...
BRAV...
SIGH. WHAT SHOULD I DO...?
TMP

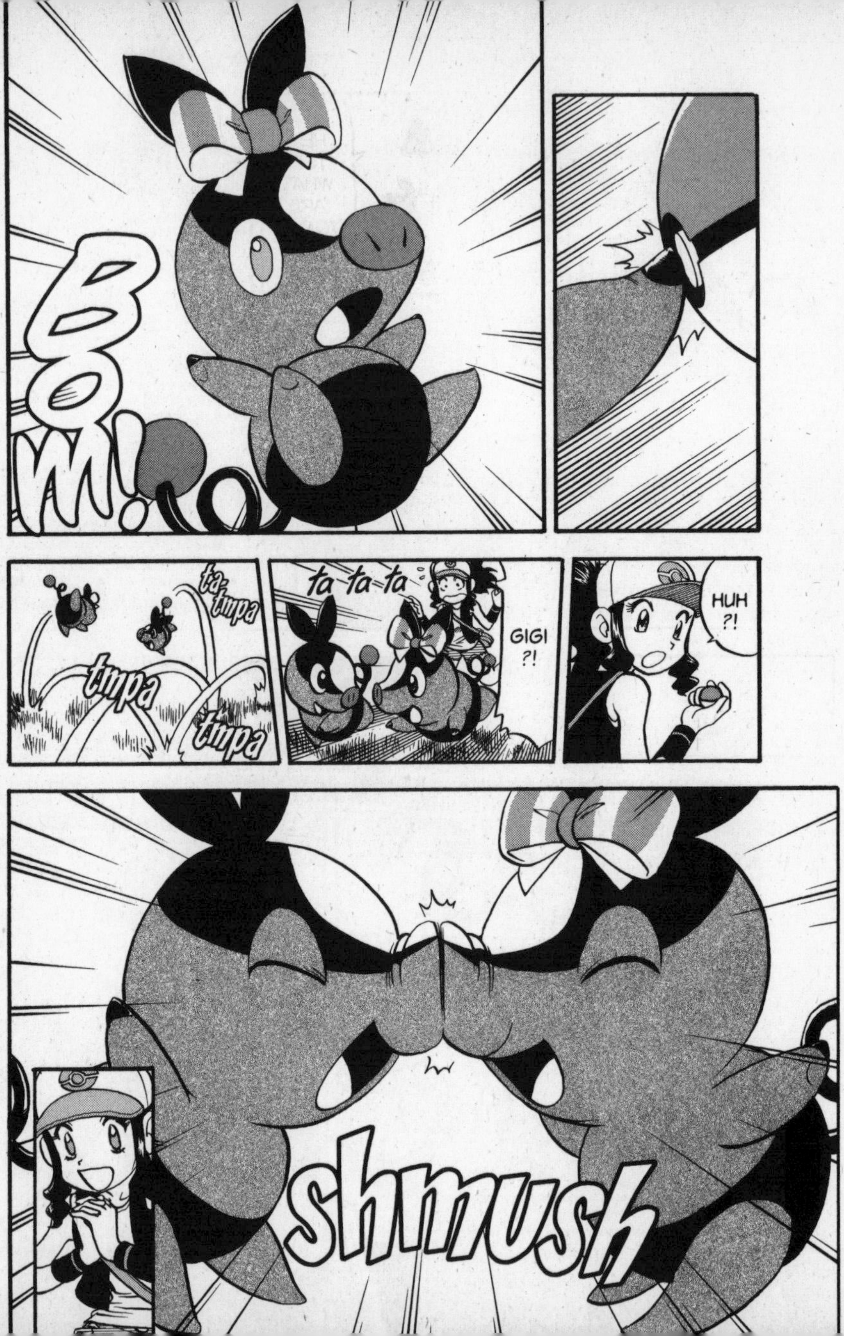
BOOM!
ta-tmpa
tmpa
tmpa
ta-ta-ta
GIGI ?!
HUH ?!
shmush

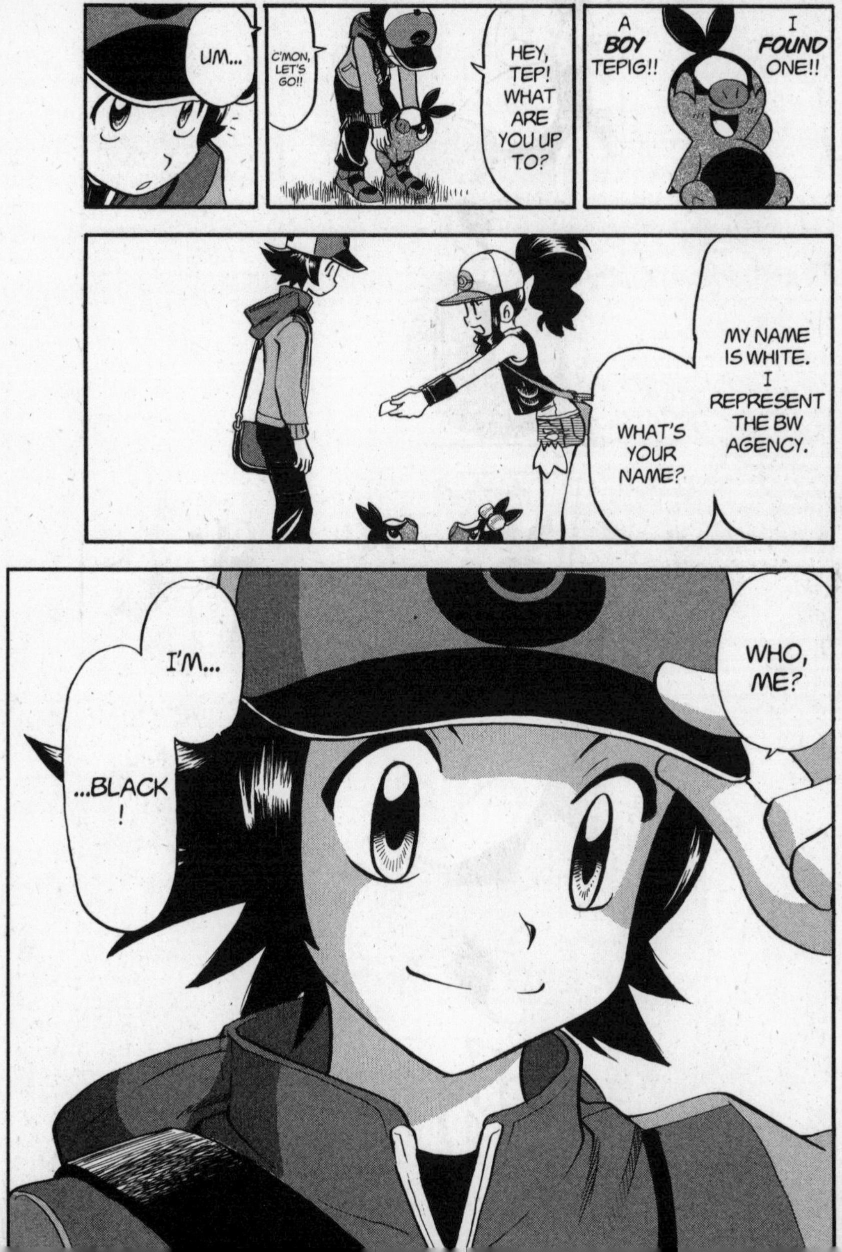
I FOUND ONE!!
A BOY TEPIG!!
HEY, TEP! WHAT ARE YOU UP TO?
C'MON, LET'S GO!!
UM...
MY NAME IS WHITE. I REPRESENT THE BW AGENCY.
WHAT'S YOUR NAME?
WHO, ME?
I'M...
...BLACK!

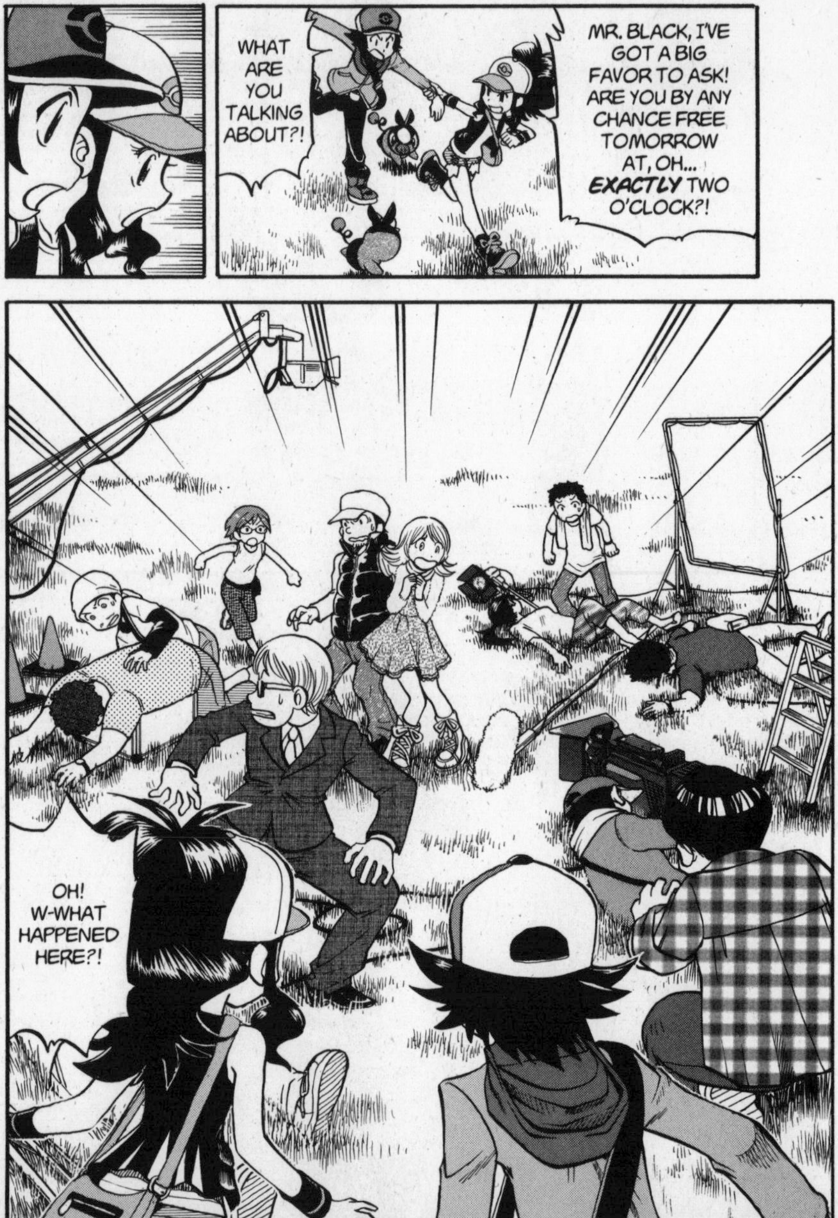
MR. BLACK, I'VE GOT A BIG FAVOR TO ASK! ARE YOU BY ANY CHANCE FREE TOMORROW AT, OH... **EXACTLY** TWO O'CLOCK?!
WHAT ARE YOU TALKING ABOUT?!
OH! W-WHAT HAPPENED HERE?!

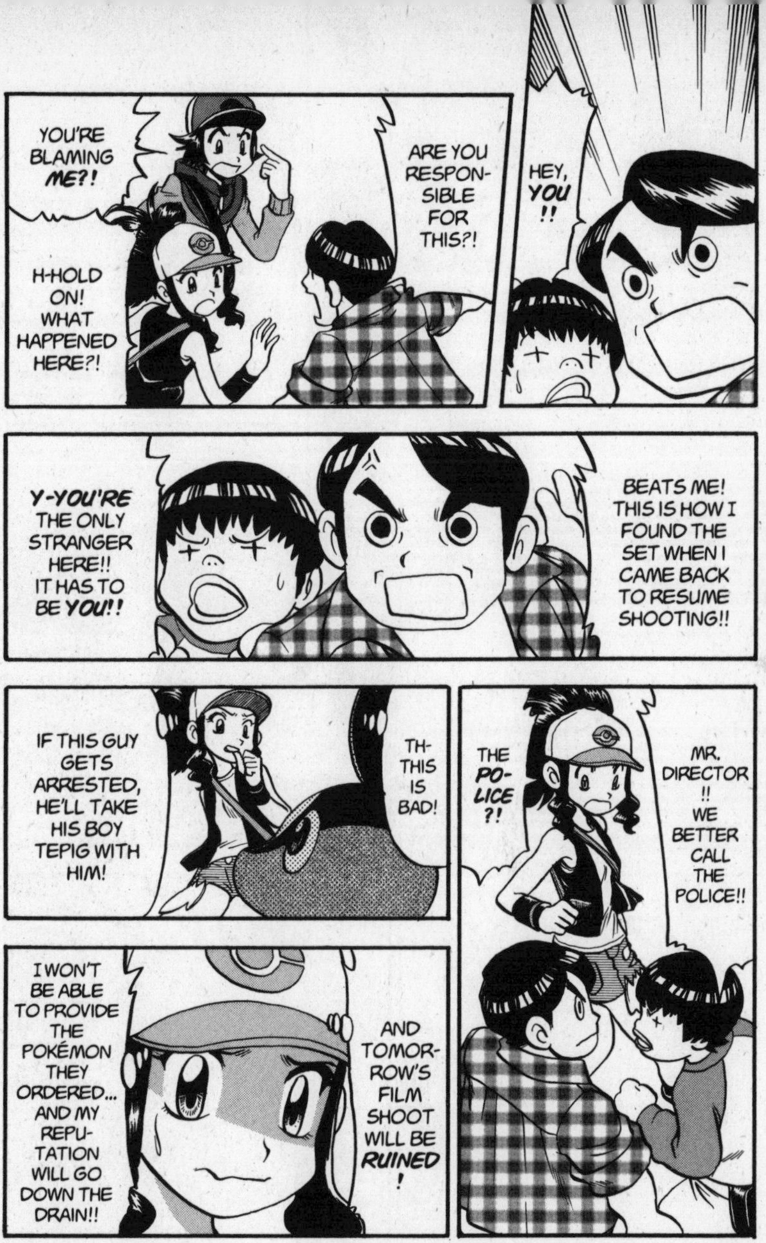

HEY, YOU!!
ARE YOU RESPONSIBLE FOR THIS?!
YOU'RE BLAMING ME?!
H-HOLD ON! WHAT HAPPENED HERE?!
BEATS ME! THIS IS HOW I FOUND THE SET WHEN I CAME BACK TO RESUME SHOOTING!!
Y-YOU'RE THE ONLY STRANGER HERE!! IT HAS TO BE YOU!!
MR. DIRECTOR!! WE BETTER CALL THE POLICE!!
THE POLICE?!
TH-THIS IS BAD!
IF THIS GUY GETS ARRESTED, HE'LL TAKE HIS BOY TEPIG WITH HIM!
AND TOMORROW'S FILM SHOOT WILL BE RUINED!
I WON'T BE ABLE TO PROVIDE THE POKÉMON THEY ORDERED... AND MY REPUTATION WILL GO DOWN THE DRAIN!!

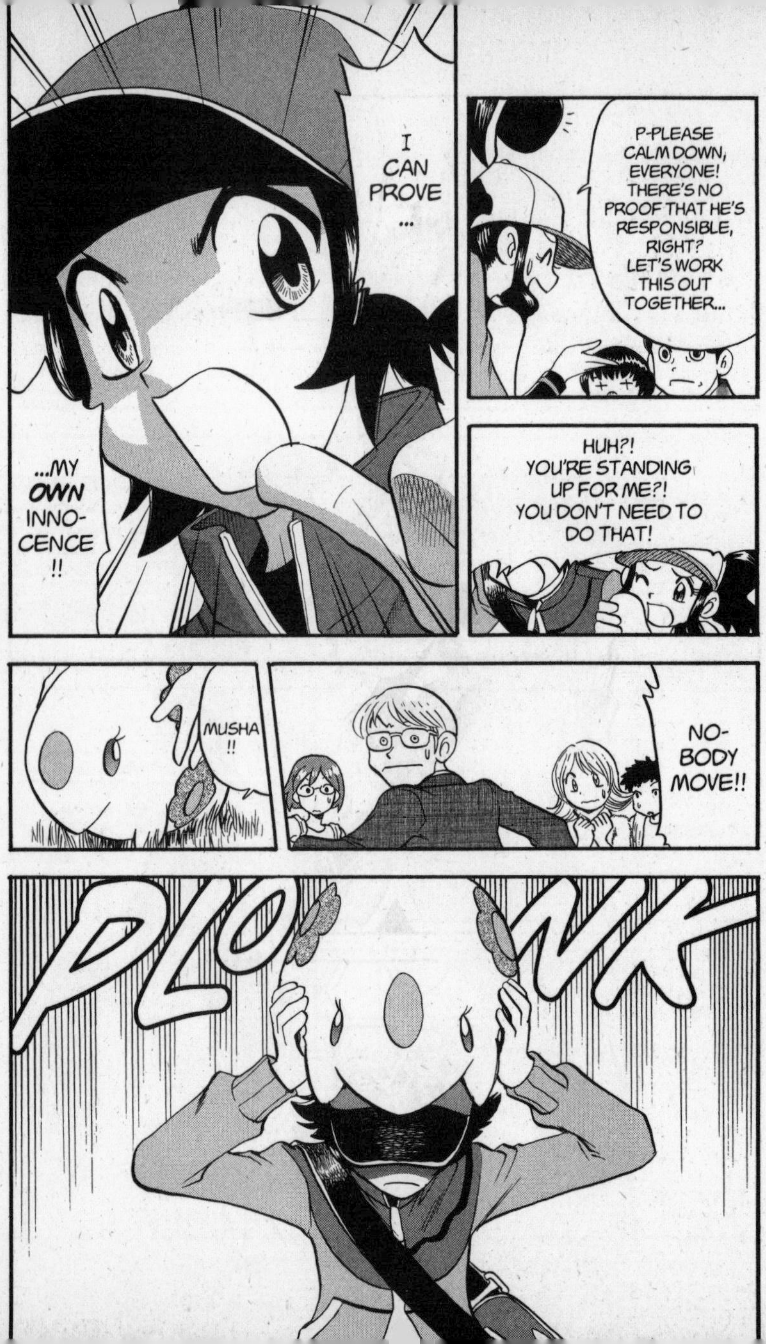
P-PLEASE CALM DOWN, EVERYONE! THERE'S NO PROOF THAT HE'S RESPONSIBLE, RIGHT? LET'S WORK THIS OUT TOGETHER...
I CAN PROVE ...
...MY OWN INNOCENCE !!
HUH?! YOU'RE STANDING UP FOR ME?! YOU DON'T NEED TO DO THAT!
NO-BODY MOVE!!
MUSHA !!
PLONK

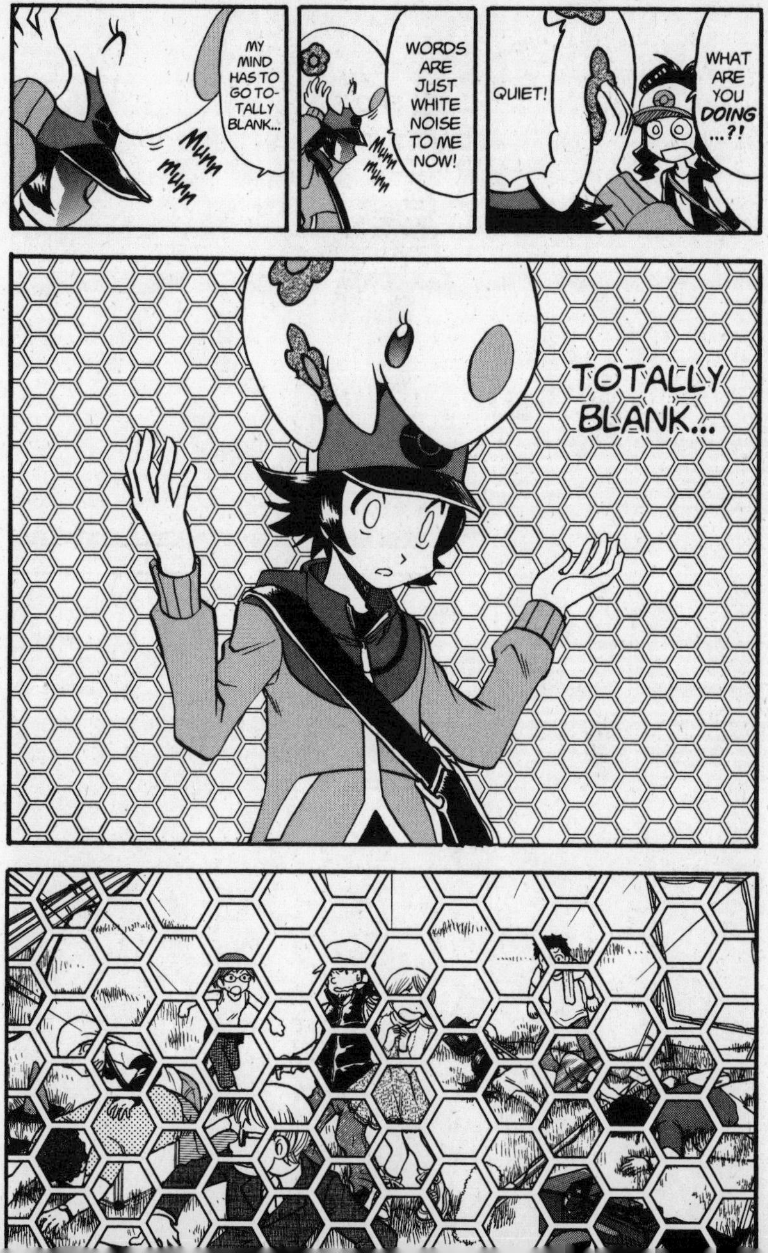

MY MIND HAS TO GO TO-TALLY BLANK...
MUMM MUMM
WORDS ARE JUST WHITE NOISE TO ME NOW!
MUMM MUMM
QUIET!
WHAT ARE YOU DOING ...?!
TOTALLY BLANK...

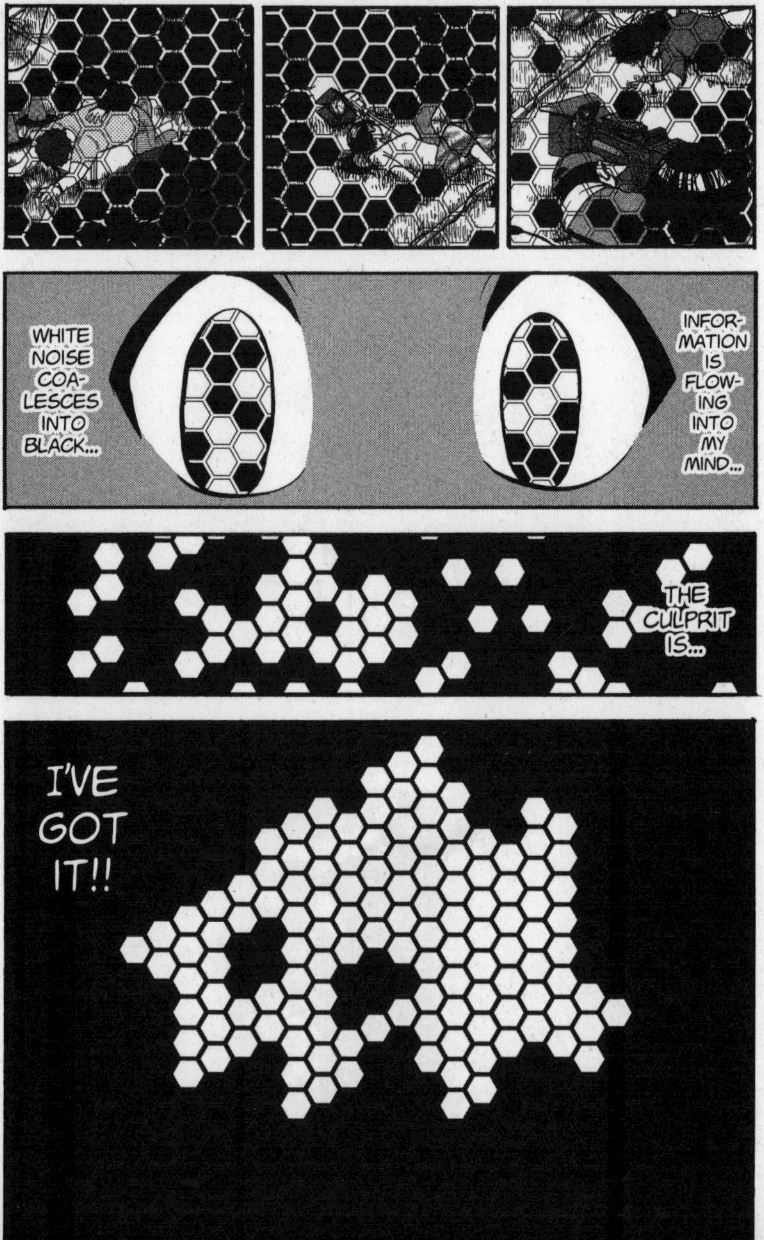
INFOR-MATION IS FLOW-ING INTO MY MIND...
WHITE NOISE COA-LESCES INTO BLACK...
THE CULPRIT IS...
I'VE GOT IT!!

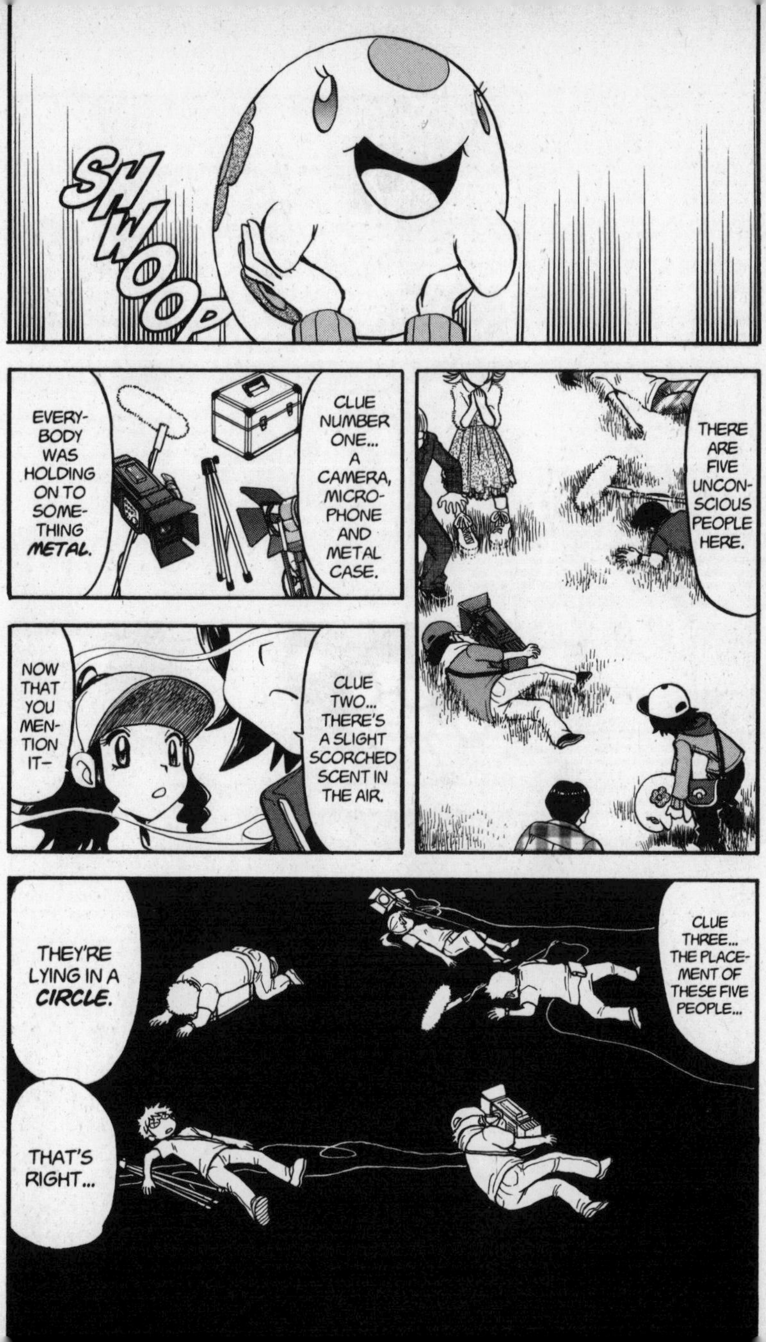
SHWOOP
CLUE NUMBER ONE... A CAMERA, MICROPHONE AND METAL CASE.
EVERYBODY WAS HOLDING ON TO SOMETHING METAL.
THERE ARE FIVE UNCONSCIOUS PEOPLE HERE.
CLUE TWO... THERE'S A SLIGHT SCORCHED SCENT IN THE AIR.
NOW THAT YOU MENTION IT—
CLUE THREE... THE PLACEMENT OF THESE FIVE PEOPLE...
THEY'RE LYING IN A CIRCLE.
THAT'S RIGHT...

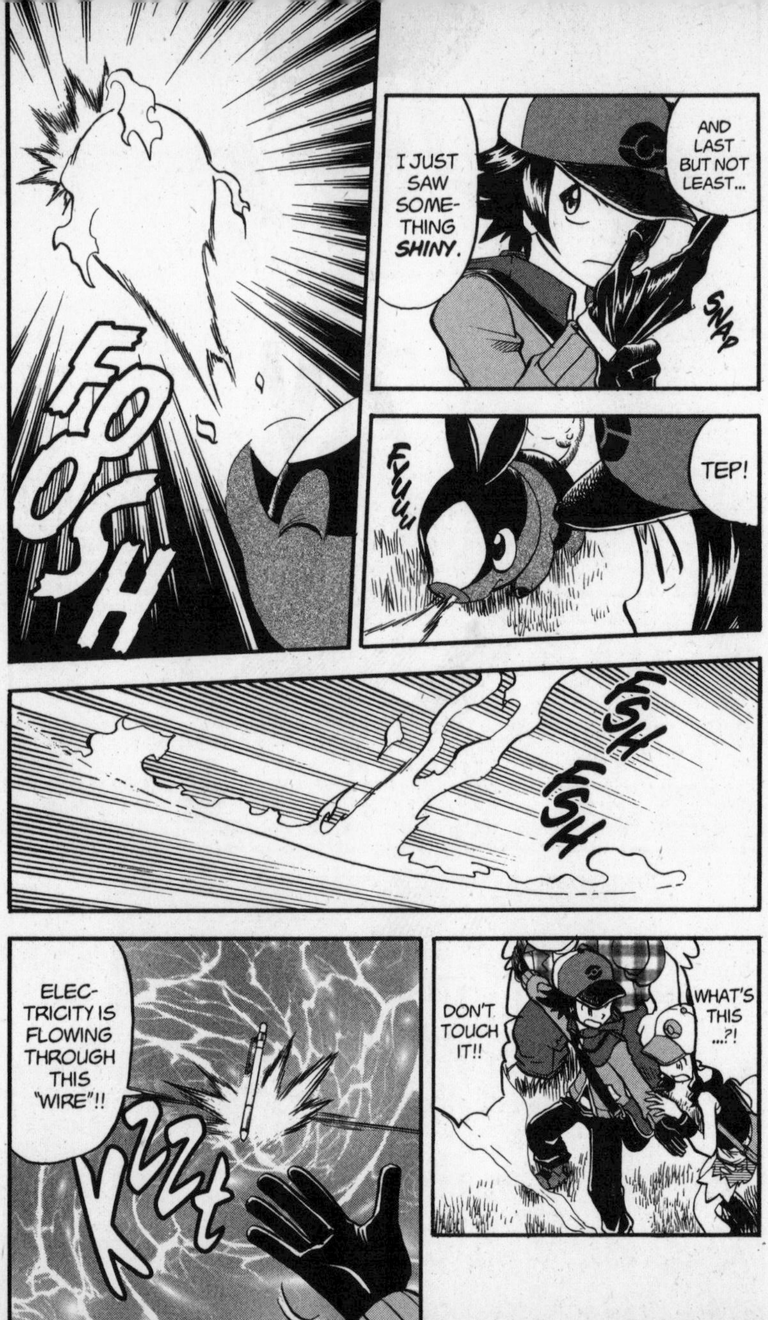
FOOSH
AND LAST BUT NOT LEAST...
I JUST SAW SOME-THING SHINY.
SNAP
TEP!
FWUUU
FSH
FSH
DON'T TOUCH IT!!
WHAT'S THIS ...?!
ELEC-TRICITY IS FLOWING THROUGH THIS "WIRE"!!
KZZZt

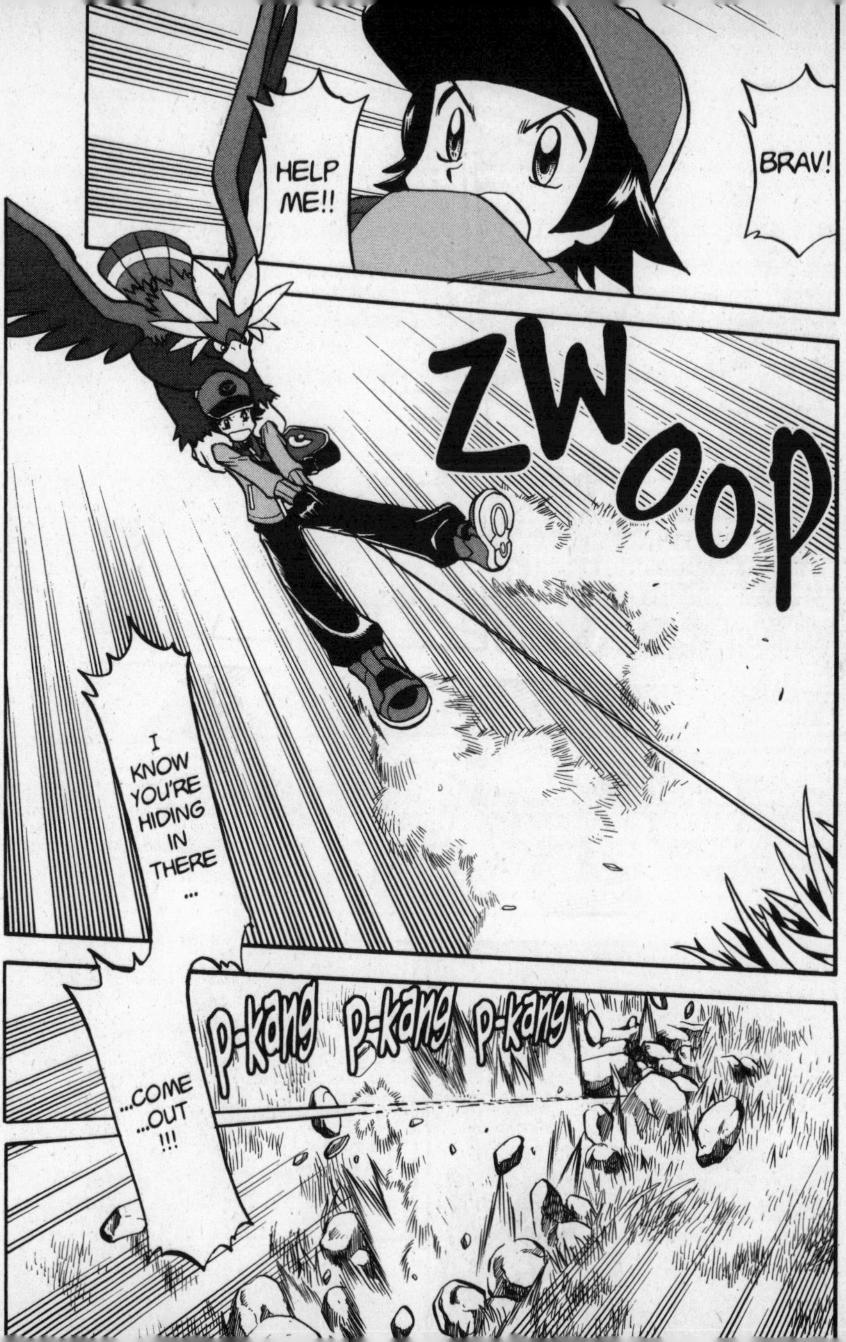
HELP ME!!
BRAV!
ZWOOP
I KNOW YOU'RE HIDING IN THERE ...
p-kang p-kang p-kang
...COME ...OUT !!!

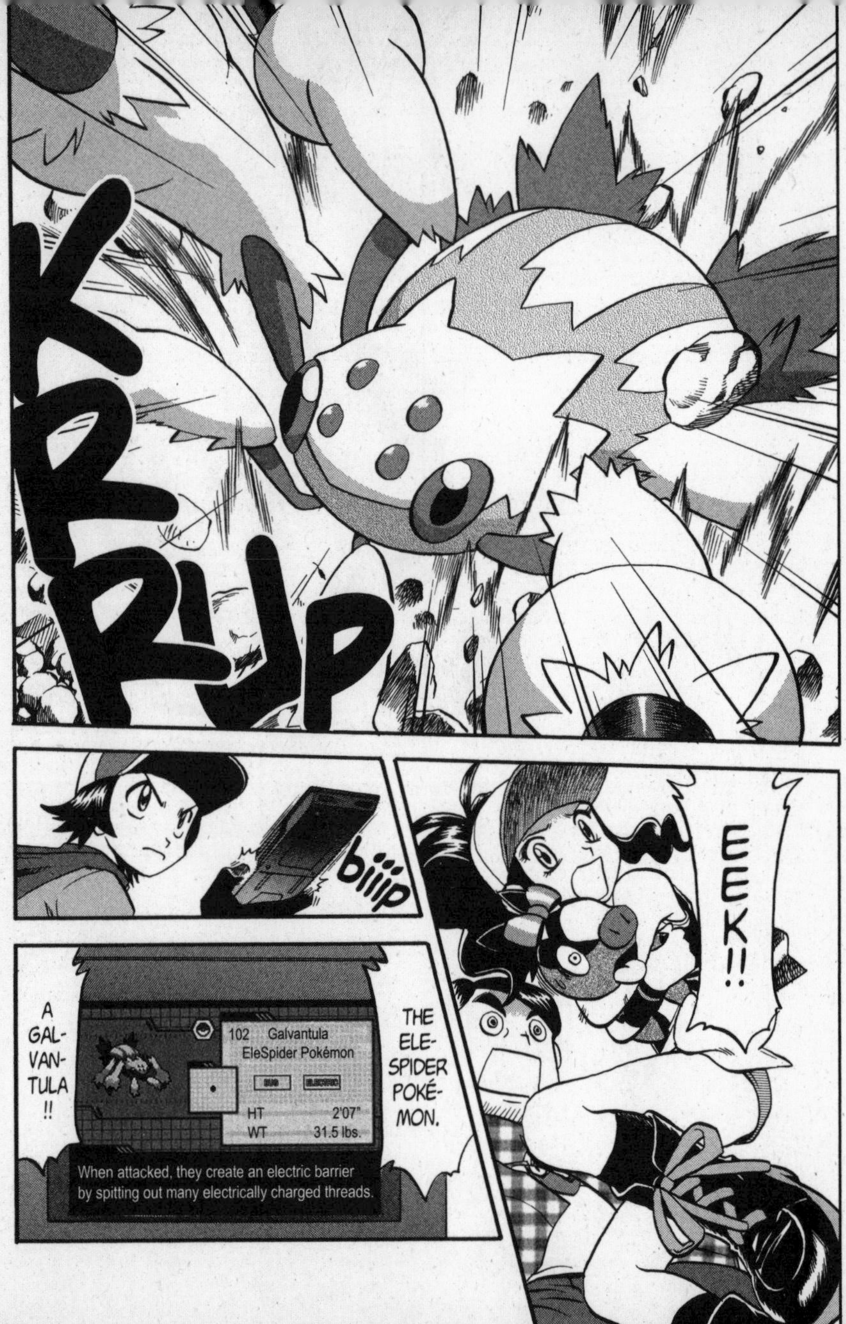
KRUP
EEEK!!
biiip
A GAL-VAN-TULA!!
THE ELE-SPIDER POKÉ-MON.
102 Galvantula
EleSpider Pokémon
HT 2'07"
WT 31.5 lbs.
When attacked, they create an electric barrier by spitting out many electrically charged threads.

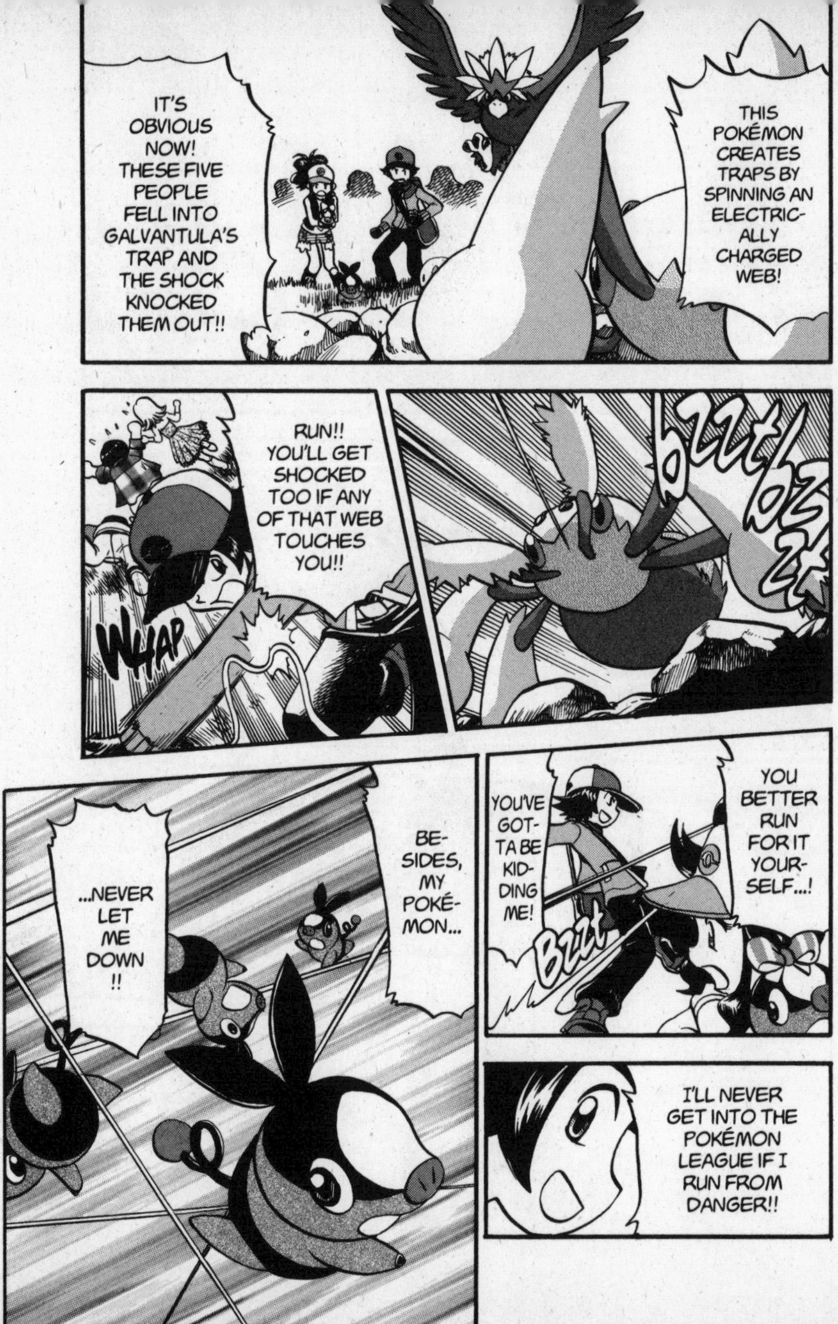
IT'S OBVIOUS NOW! THESE FIVE PEOPLE FELL INTO GALVANTULA'S TRAP AND THE SHOCK KNOCKED THEM OUT!!
THIS POKÉMON CREATES TRAPS BY SPINNING AN ELECTRIC-ALLY CHARGED WEB!
RUN!! YOU'LL GET SHOCKED TOO IF ANY OF THAT WEB TOUCHES YOU!!
WHAP
bzzt bzzt
YOU BETTER RUN FOR IT YOUR-SELF...!
YOU'VE GOT-TA BE KID-DING ME!
Bzzt
I'LL NEVER GET INTO THE POKÉMON LEAGUE IF I RUN FROM DANGER!!
BE-SIDES, MY POKÉ-MON...
...NEVER LET ME DOWN !!

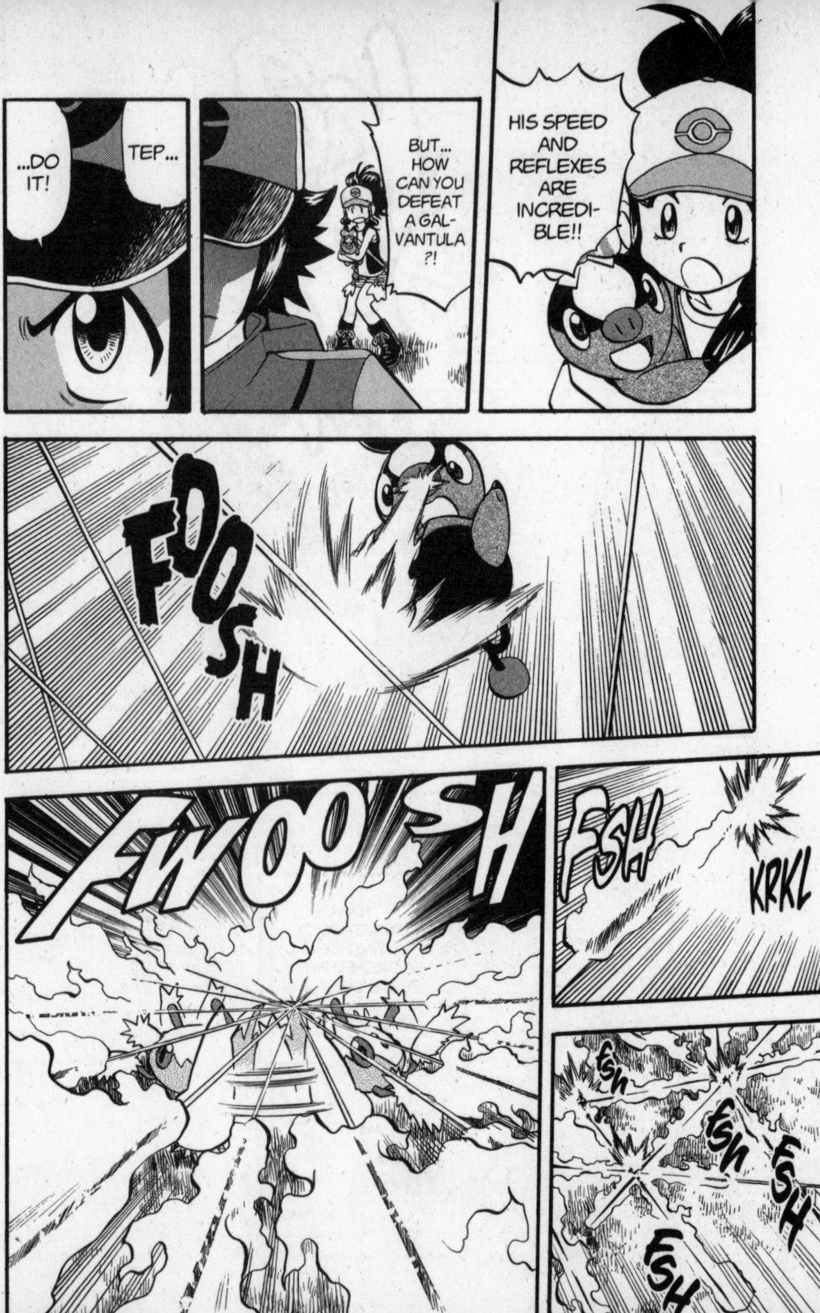
HIS SPEED AND REFLEXES ARE INCREDIBLE!!
BUT... HOW CAN YOU DEFEAT A GALVANTULA ?!
TEP...
...DO IT!
FOOSH
FWOOSH
FSH
KRKL
FSH
FSH
FSH
FSH
FSH

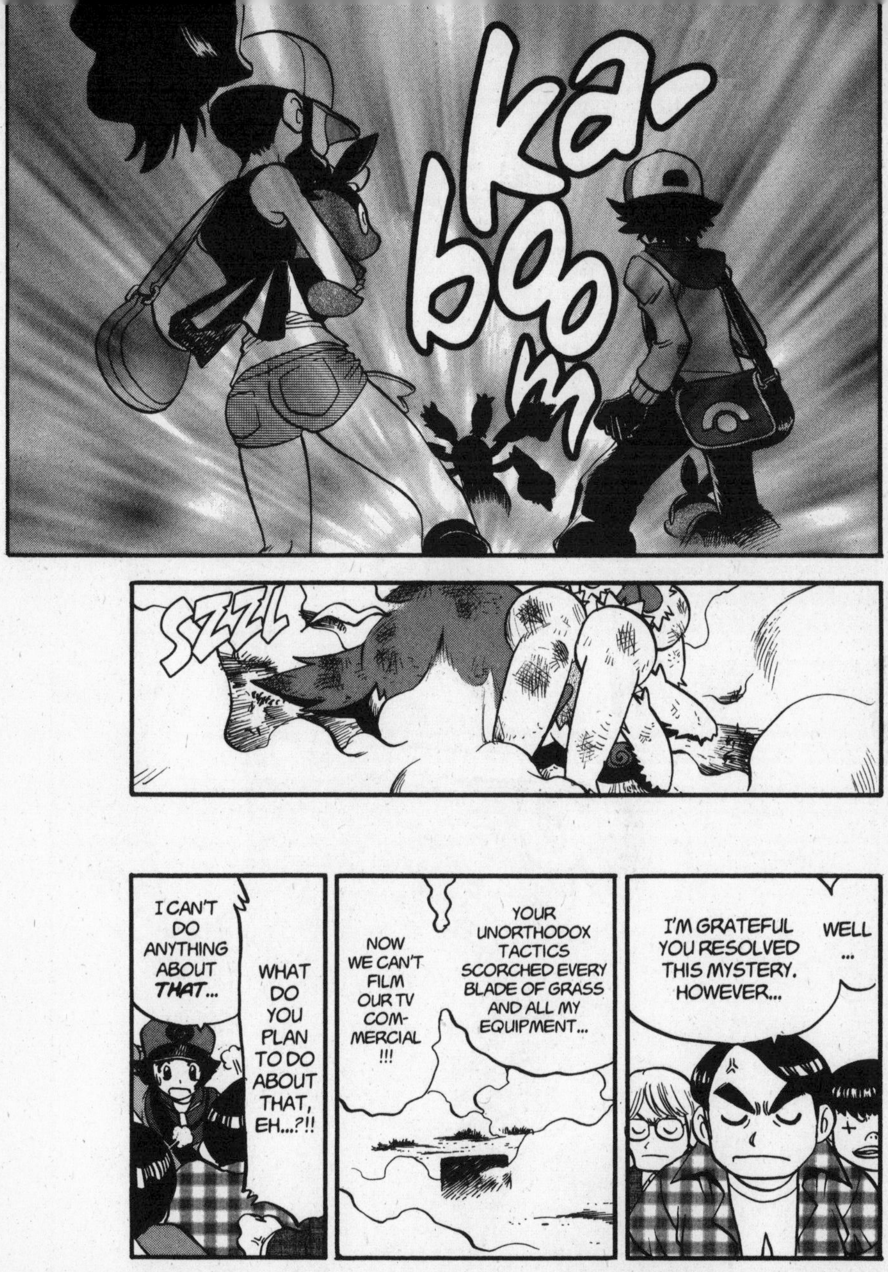
KA-BOOOM
SZZZ
WELL ...
I'M GRATEFUL YOU RESOLVED THIS MYSTERY. HOWEVER...
YOUR UNORTHODOX TACTICS SCORCHED EVERY BLADE OF GRASS AND ALL MY EQUIPMENT...
NOW WE CAN'T FILM OUR TV COM-MERCIAL !!!
WHAT DO YOU PLAN TO DO ABOUT THAT, EH...?!!
I CAN'T DO ANYTHING ABOUT *THAT*...

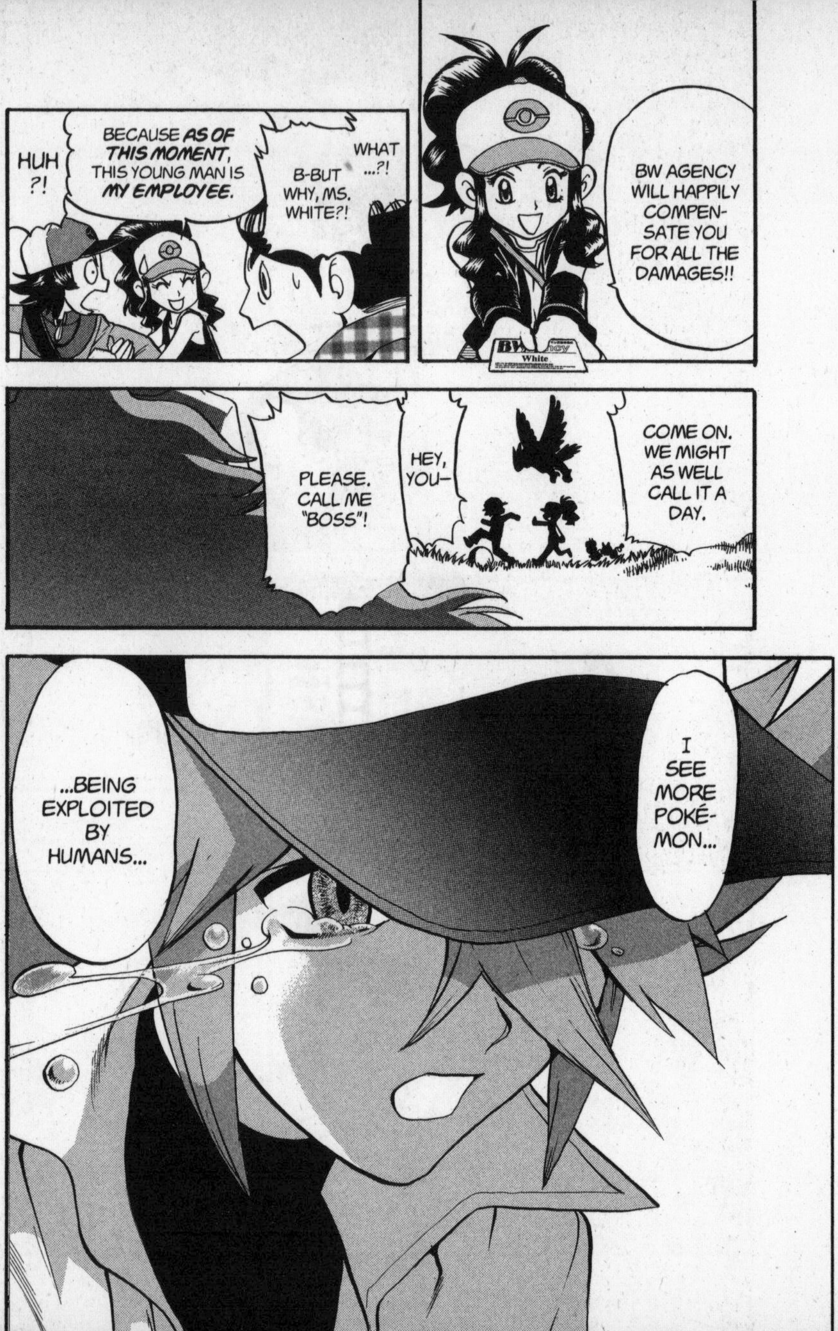
BW AGENCY WILL HAPPILY COMPENSATE YOU FOR ALL THE DAMAGES!!
BW Agency
White
WHAT ...?!
B-BUT WHY, MS. WHITE?!
BECAUSE AS OF THIS MOMENT, THIS YOUNG MAN IS MY EMPLOYEE.
HUH ?!
COME ON. WE MIGHT AS WELL CALL IT A DAY.
HEY, YOU—
PLEASE. CALL ME "BOSS"!
I SEE MORE POKÉMON...
...BEING EXPLOITED BY HUMANS...

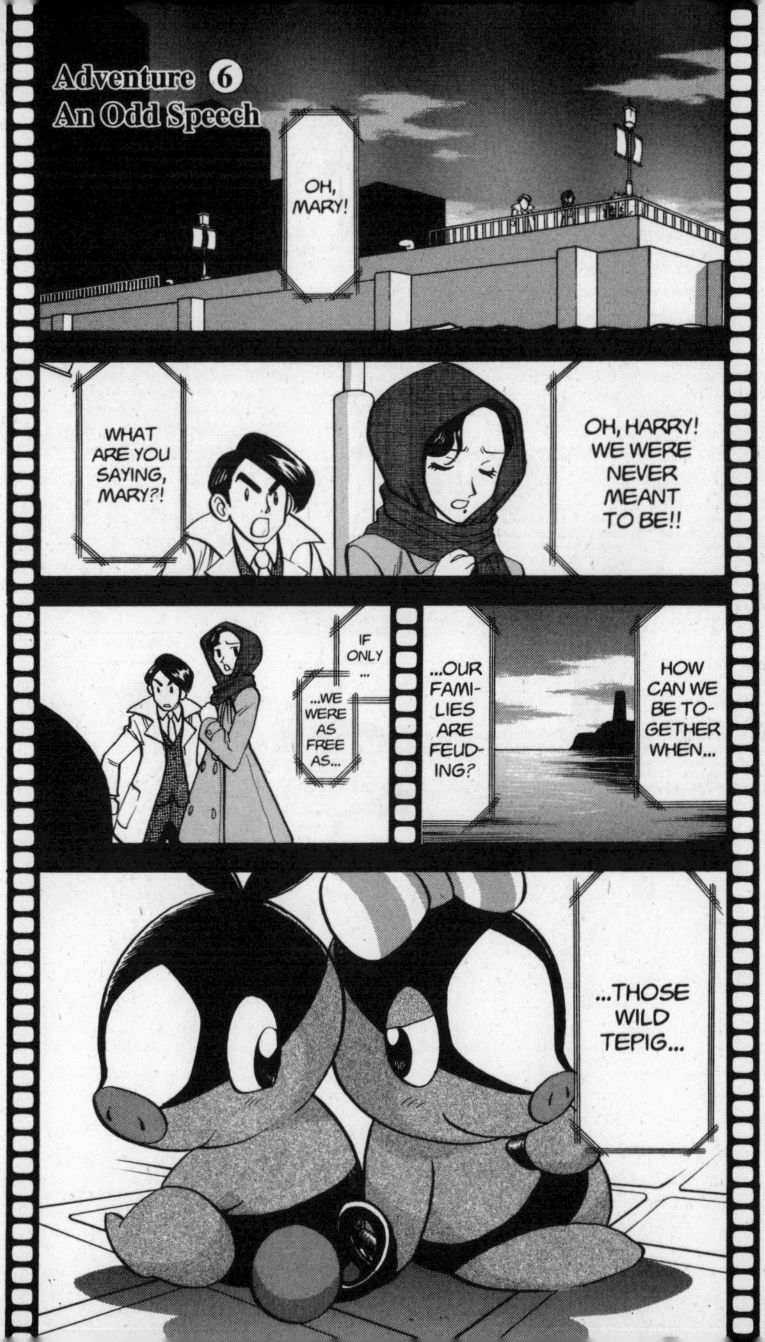
Adventure 6
An Odd Speech
OH, MARY!
OH, HARRY! WE WERE NEVER MEANT TO BE!!
WHAT ARE YOU SAYING, MARY?!
HOW CAN WE BE TO-GETHER WHEN...
...OUR FAMI-LIES ARE FEUD-ING?
IF ONLY...
...WE WERE AS FREE AS...
...THOSE WILD TEPIG...

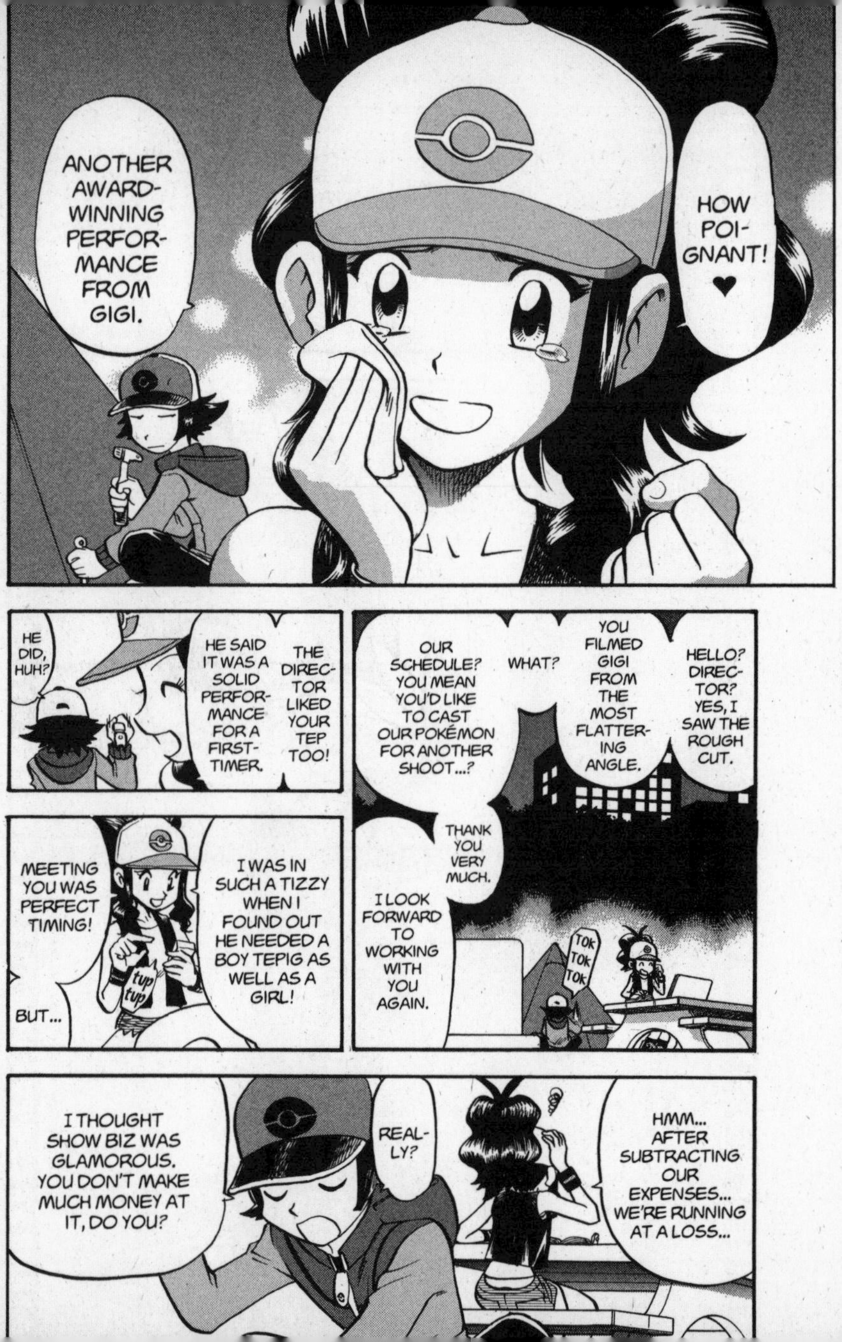
HOW POIGNANT! ♥
ANOTHER AWARD-WINNING PERFORMANCE FROM GIGI.
HELLO? DIRECTOR? YES, I SAW THE ROUGH CUT.
YOU FILMED GIGI FROM THE MOST FLATTERING ANGLE.
WHAT?
OUR SCHEDULE? YOU MEAN YOU'D LIKE TO CAST OUR POKÉMON FOR ANOTHER SHOOT...?
THANK YOU VERY MUCH.
I LOOK FORWARD TO WORKING WITH YOU AGAIN.
TOK TOK TOK
THE DIRECTOR LIKED YOUR TEP TOO!
HE SAID IT WAS A SOLID PERFORMANCE FOR A FIRST-TIMER.
HE DID, HUH?
I WAS IN SUCH A TIZZY WHEN I FOUND OUT HE NEEDED A BOY TEPIG AS WELL AS A GIRL!
tup tup
MEETING YOU WAS PERFECT TIMING!
BUT...
HMM... AFTER SUBTRACTING OUR EXPENSES... WE'RE RUNNING AT A LOSS...
REALLY?
I THOUGHT SHOW BIZ WAS GLAMOROUS. YOU DON'T MAKE MUCH MONEY AT IT, DO YOU?

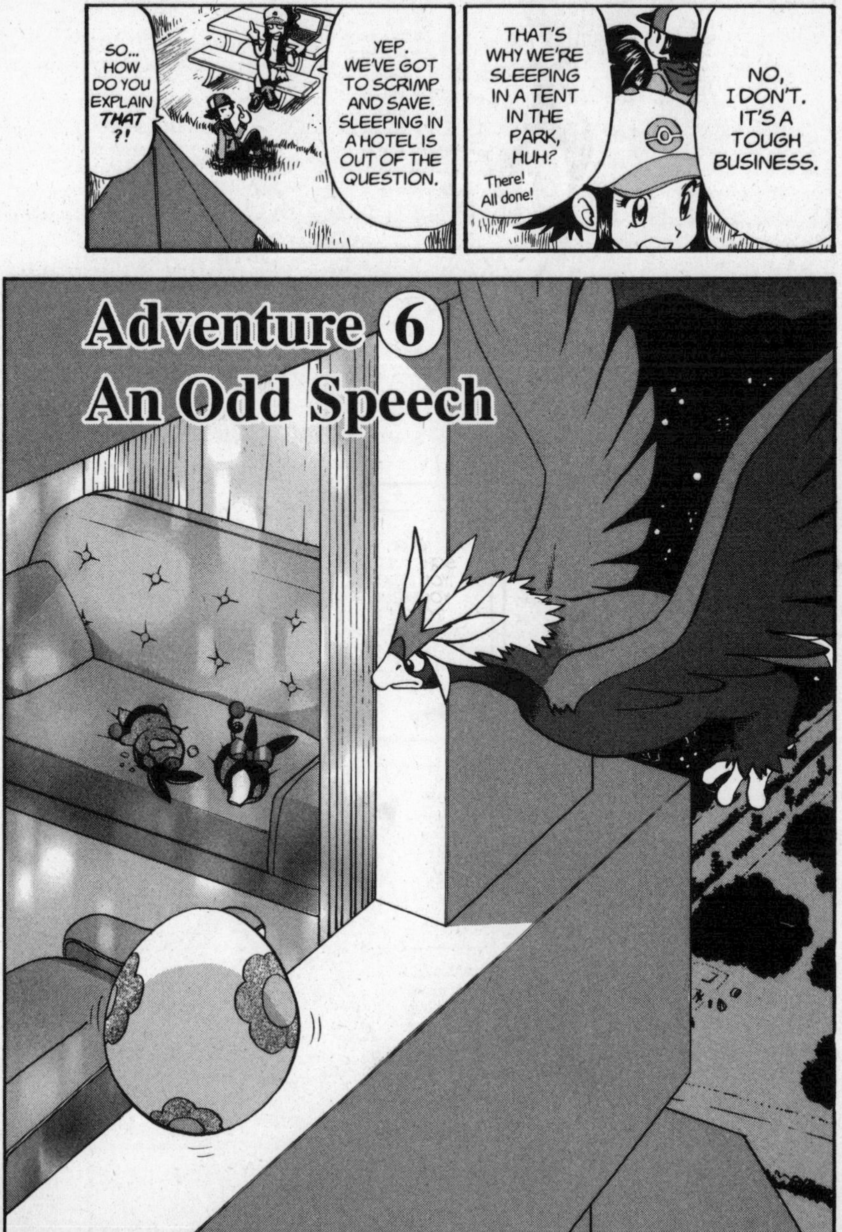
NO, I DON'T. IT'S A TOUGH BUSINESS.
THAT'S WHY WE'RE SLEEPING IN A TENT IN THE PARK, HUH?
There! All done!
YEP. WE'VE GOT TO SCRIMP AND SAVE. SLEEPING IN A HOTEL IS OUT OF THE QUESTION.
SO... HOW DO YOU EXPLAIN THAT?!
Adventure 6
An Odd Speech

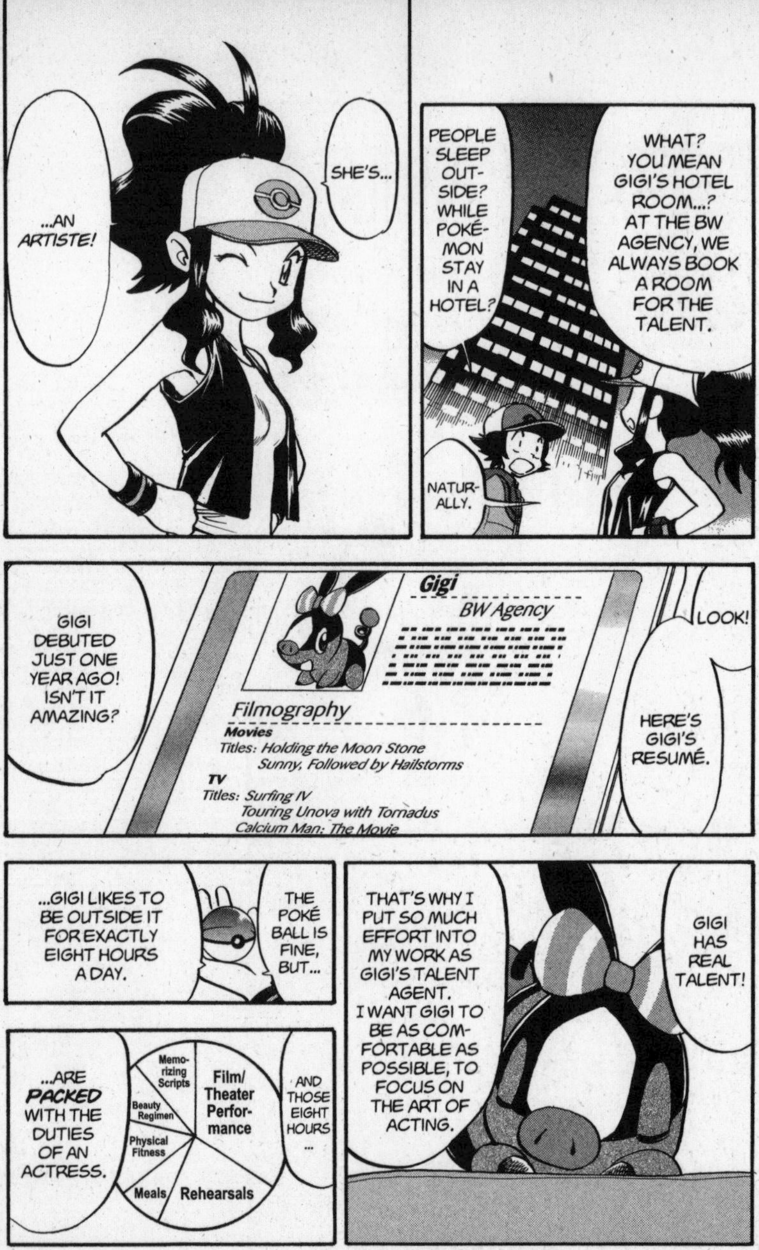

WHAT? YOU MEAN GIGI'S HOTEL ROOM...? AT THE BW AGENCY, WE ALWAYS BOOK A ROOM FOR THE TALENT.
PEOPLE SLEEP OUTSIDE? WHILE POKÉMON STAY IN A HOTEL?
NATURALLY.
SHE'S...
...AN ARTISTE!
LOOK!
HERE'S GIGI'S RESUMÉ.
Gigi
BW Agency
Filmography
Movies
Titles: Holding the Moon Stone
Sunny, Followed by Hailstorms
TV
Titles: Surfing IV
Touring Unova with Tornadus
Calcium Man: The Movie
GIGI DEBUTED JUST ONE YEAR AGO! ISN'T IT AMAZING?
GIGI HAS REAL TALENT!
THAT'S WHY I PUT SO MUCH EFFORT INTO MY WORK AS GIGI'S TALENT AGENT. I WANT GIGI TO BE AS COMFORTABLE AS POSSIBLE, TO FOCUS ON THE ART OF ACTING.
THE POKÉ BALL IS FINE, BUT...
...GIGI LIKES TO BE OUTSIDE IT FOR EXACTLY EIGHT HOURS A DAY.
AND THOSE EIGHT HOURS...
...ARE PACKED WITH THE DUTIES OF AN ACTRESS.
Memorizing Scripts
Film/ Theater Performance
Beauty Regimen
Physical Fitness
Meals
Rehearsals

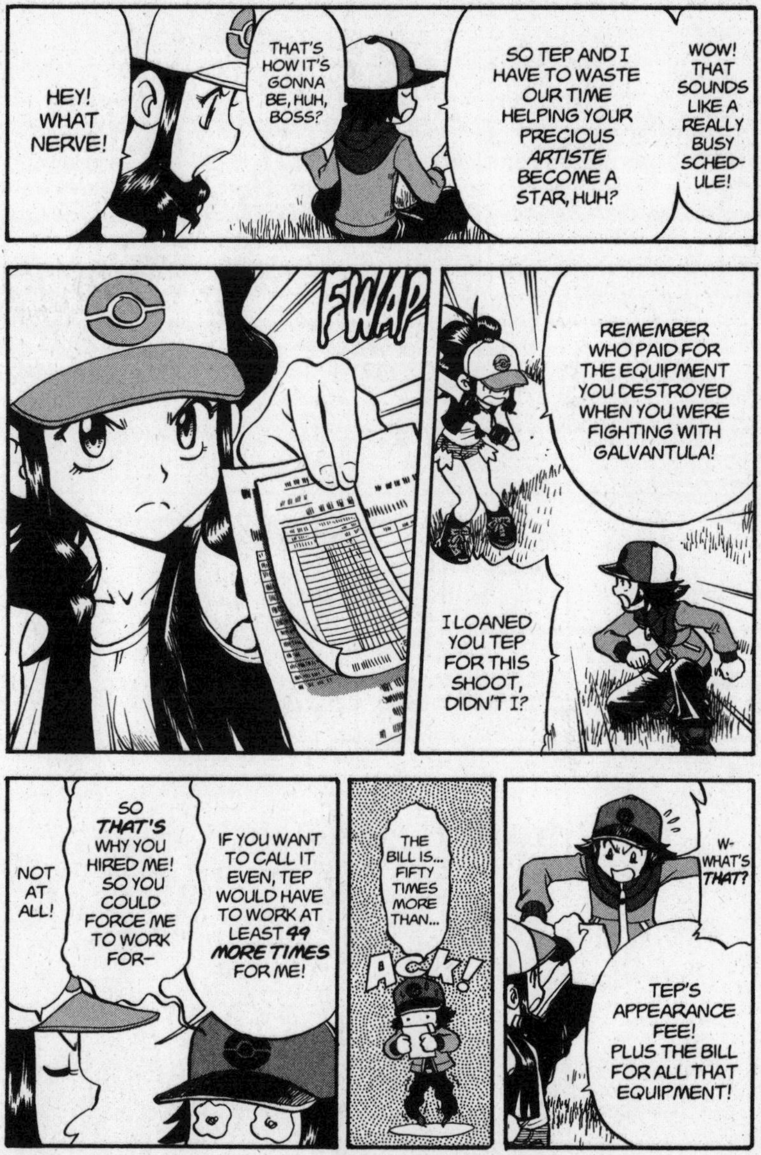
WOW! THAT SOUNDS LIKE A REALLY BUSY SCHED-ULE!
SO TEP AND I HAVE TO WASTE OUR TIME HELPING YOUR PRECIOUS *ARTISTE* BECOME A STAR, HUH?
THAT'S HOW IT'S GONNA BE, HUH, BOSS?
HEY! WHAT NERVE!
REMEMBER WHO PAID FOR THE EQUIPMENT YOU DESTROYED WHEN YOU WERE FIGHTING WITH GALVANTULA!
I LOANED YOU TEP FOR THIS SHOOT, DIDN'T I?
FWAP
W-WHAT'S ***THAT?***
TEP'S APPEARANCE FEE! PLUS THE BILL FOR ALL THAT EQUIPMENT!
THE BILL IS... FIFTY TIMES MORE THAN...
ACK!
IF YOU WANT TO CALL IT EVEN, TEP WOULD HAVE TO WORK AT LEAST ***49 MORE TIMES*** FOR ME!
SO ***THAT'S*** WHY YOU HIRED ME! SO YOU COULD FORCE ME TO WORK FOR–
NOT AT ALL!

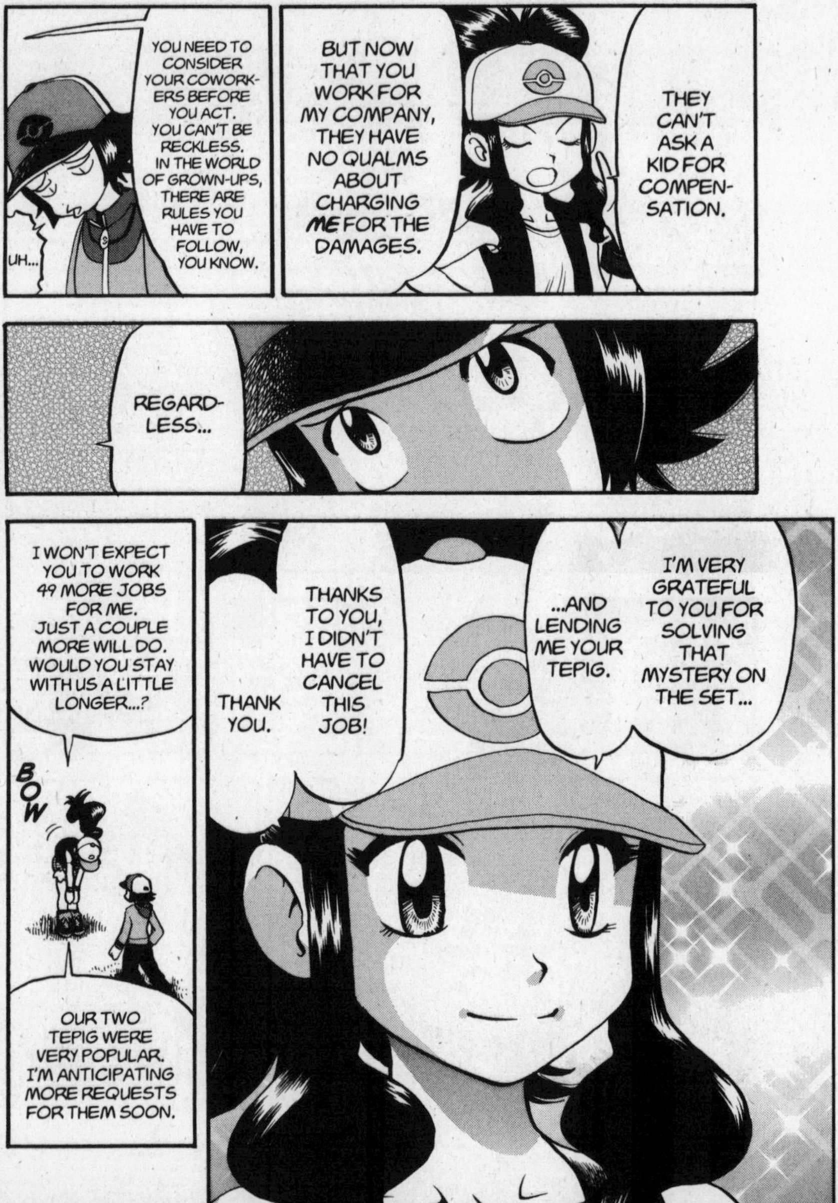
THEY CAN'T ASK A KID FOR COMPEN-SATION.
BUT NOW THAT YOU WORK FOR MY COMPANY, THEY HAVE NO QUALMS ABOUT CHARGING ME FOR THE DAMAGES.
YOU NEED TO CONSIDER YOUR COWORK-ERS BEFORE YOU ACT. YOU CAN'T BE RECKLESS. IN THE WORLD OF GROWN-UPS, THERE ARE RULES YOU HAVE TO FOLLOW, YOU KNOW.
UH...
REGARD-LESS...
I'M VERY GRATEFUL TO YOU FOR SOLVING THAT MYSTERY ON THE SET...
...AND LENDING ME YOUR TEPIG.
THANKS TO YOU, I DIDN'T HAVE TO CANCEL THIS JOB!
THANK YOU.
I WON'T EXPECT YOU TO WORK 49 MORE JOBS FOR ME. JUST A COUPLE MORE WILL DO. WOULD YOU STAY WITH US A LITTLE LONGER...?
BOW
OUR TWO TEPIG WERE VERY POPULAR. I'M ANTICIPATING MORE REQUESTS FOR THEM SOON.

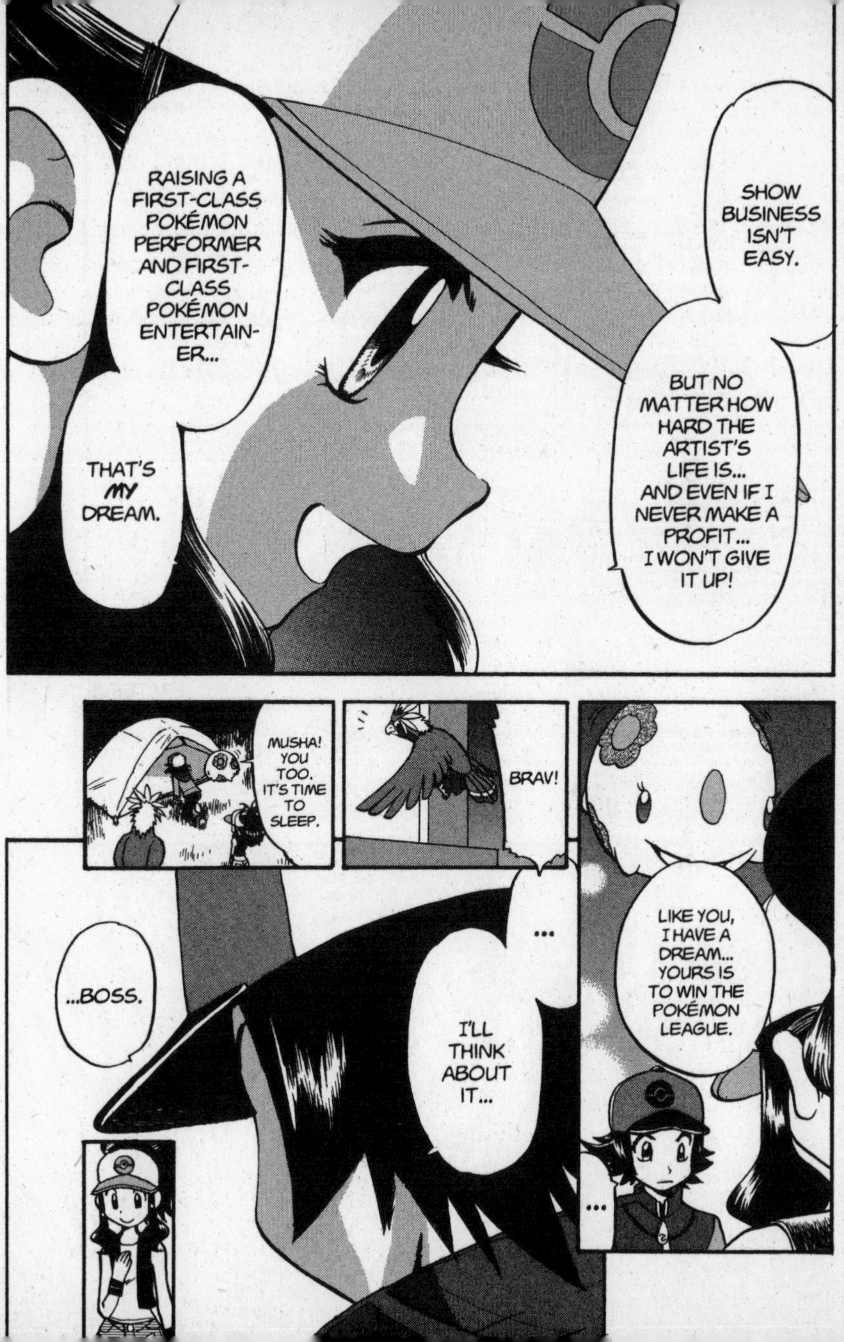
RAISING A FIRST-CLASS POKÉMON PERFORMER AND FIRST-CLASS POKÉMON ENTERTAIN-ER...
THAT'S *MY* DREAM.
SHOW BUSINESS ISN'T EASY.
BUT NO MATTER HOW HARD THE ARTIST'S LIFE IS... AND EVEN IF I NEVER MAKE A PROFIT... I WON'T GIVE IT UP!
MUSHA! YOU TOO. IT'S TIME TO SLEEP.
BRAV!
LIKE YOU, I HAVE A DREAM... YOURS IS TO WIN THE POKÉMON LEAGUE.
...
...BOSS.
...
I'LL THINK ABOUT IT...

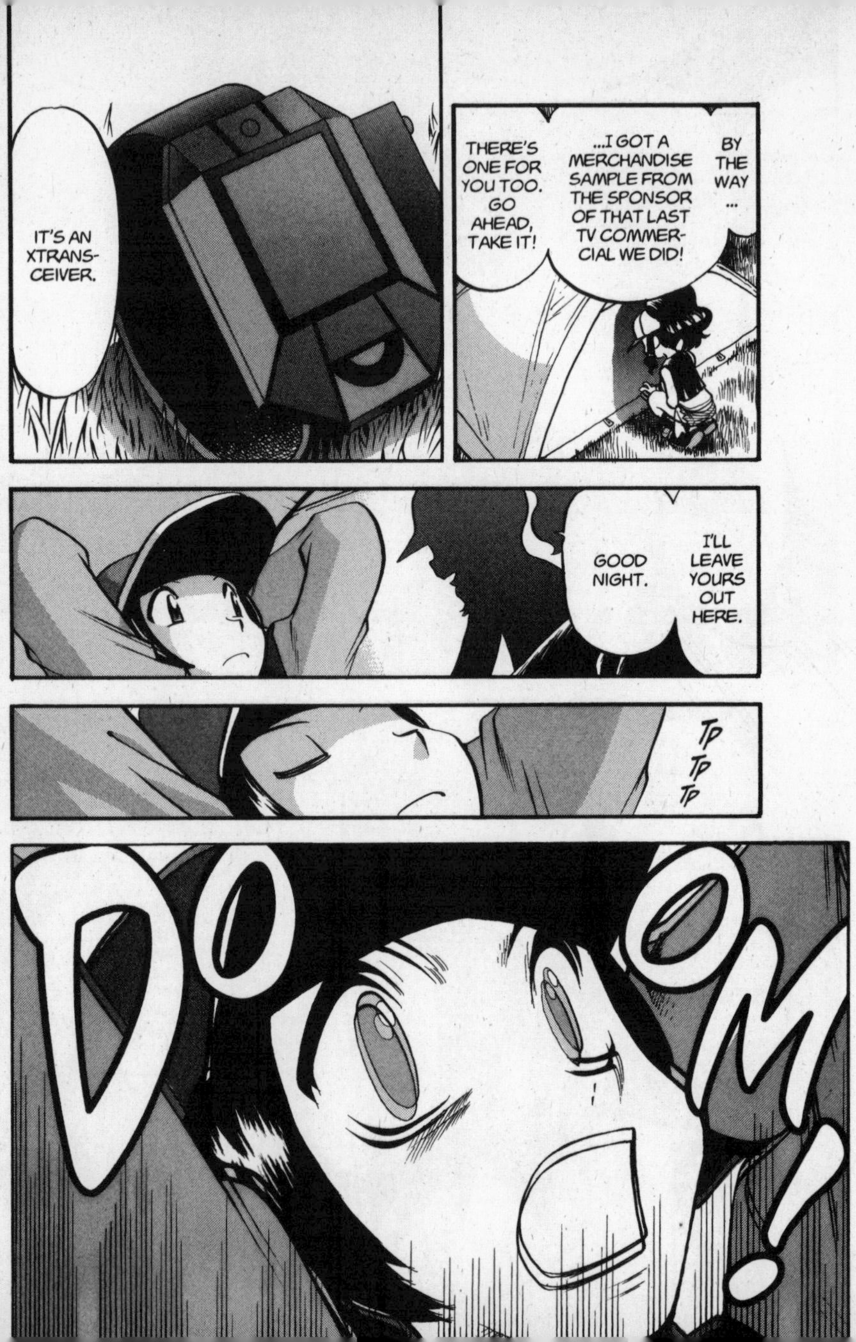
BY THE WAY ...
...I GOT A MERCHANDISE SAMPLE FROM THE SPONSOR OF THAT LAST TV COMMERCIAL WE DID!
THERE'S ONE FOR YOU TOO. GO AHEAD, TAKE IT!
IT'S AN XTRANSCEIVER.
I'LL LEAVE YOURS OUT HERE.
GOOD NIGHT.
TP TP TP
DOOM!

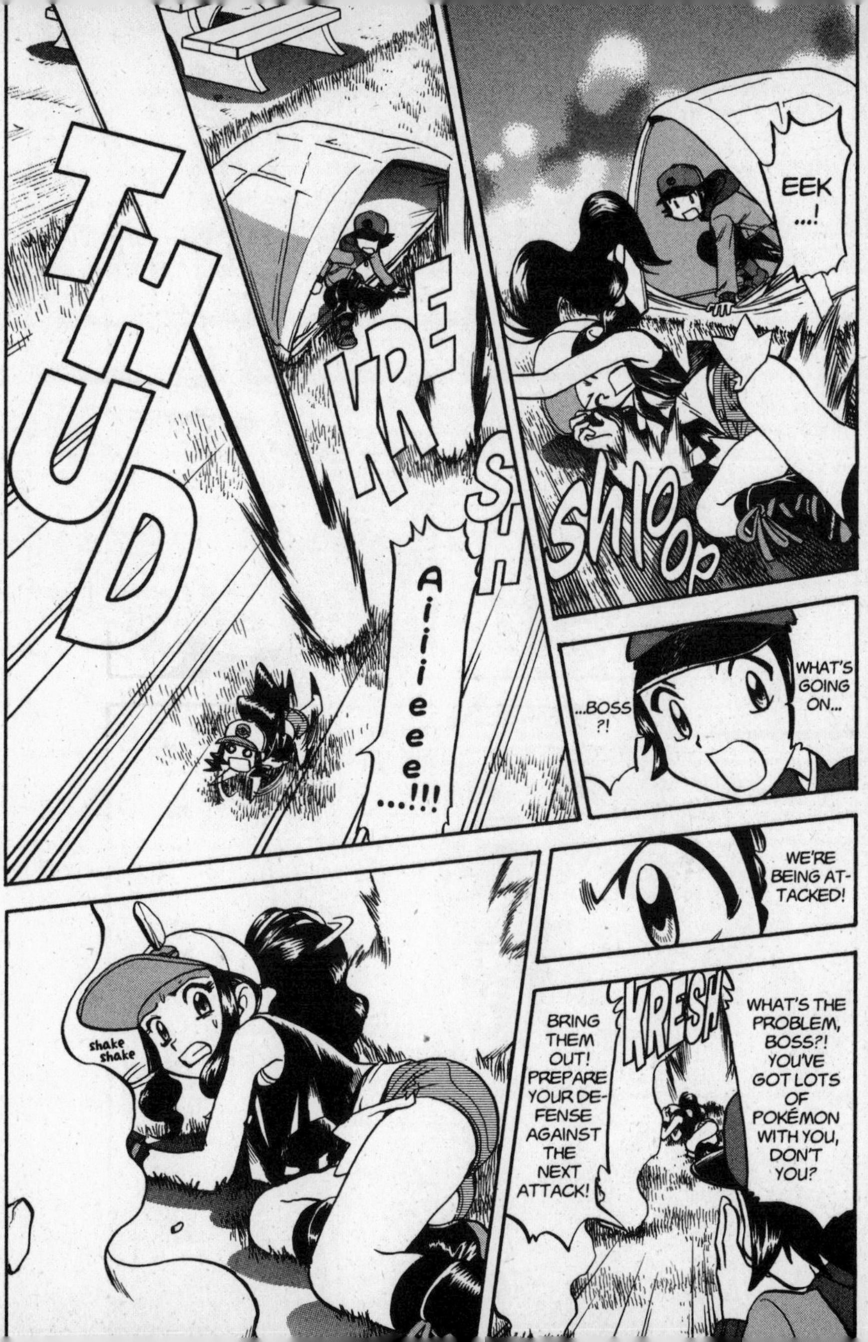

EEK ...!
SHIOOP
THUD
KRESH
Aiiiieee ...!!!
WHAT'S GOING ON...
...BOSS ?!
WE'RE BEING AT-TACKED!
WHAT'S THE PROBLEM, BOSS?! YOU'VE GOT LOTS OF POKÉMON WITH YOU, DON'T YOU?
KRESH
BRING THEM OUT! PREPARE YOUR DE-FENSE AGAINST THE NEXT ATTACK!
shake shake

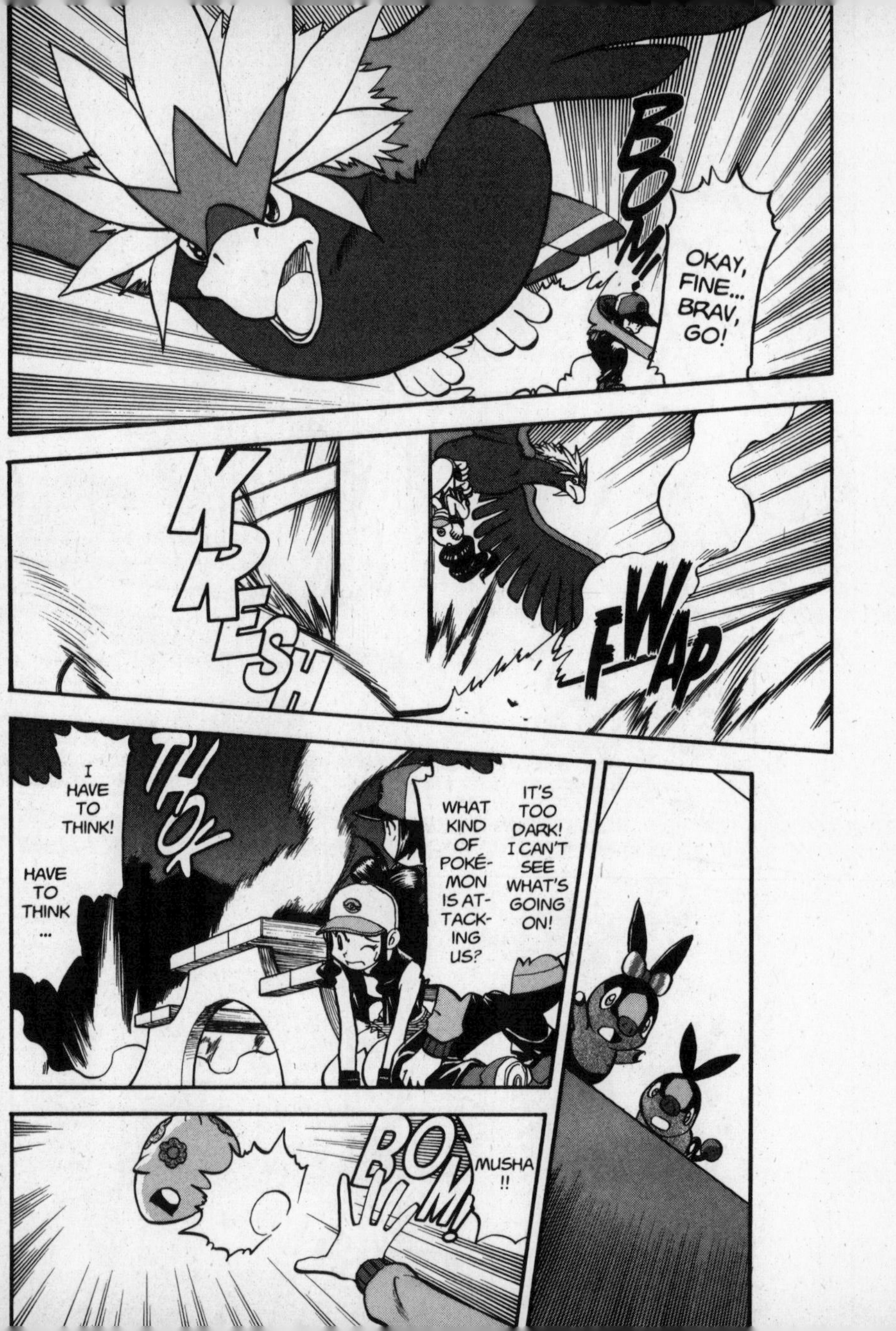
BOOM!
OKAY, FINE... BRAV, GO!
KRESH
FWAP
THOK
I HAVE TO THINK!
HAVE TO THINK ...
WHAT KIND OF POKÉMON IS ATTACKING US?
IT'S TOO DARK! I CAN'T SEE WHAT'S GOING ON!
BOOM!
MUSHA !!

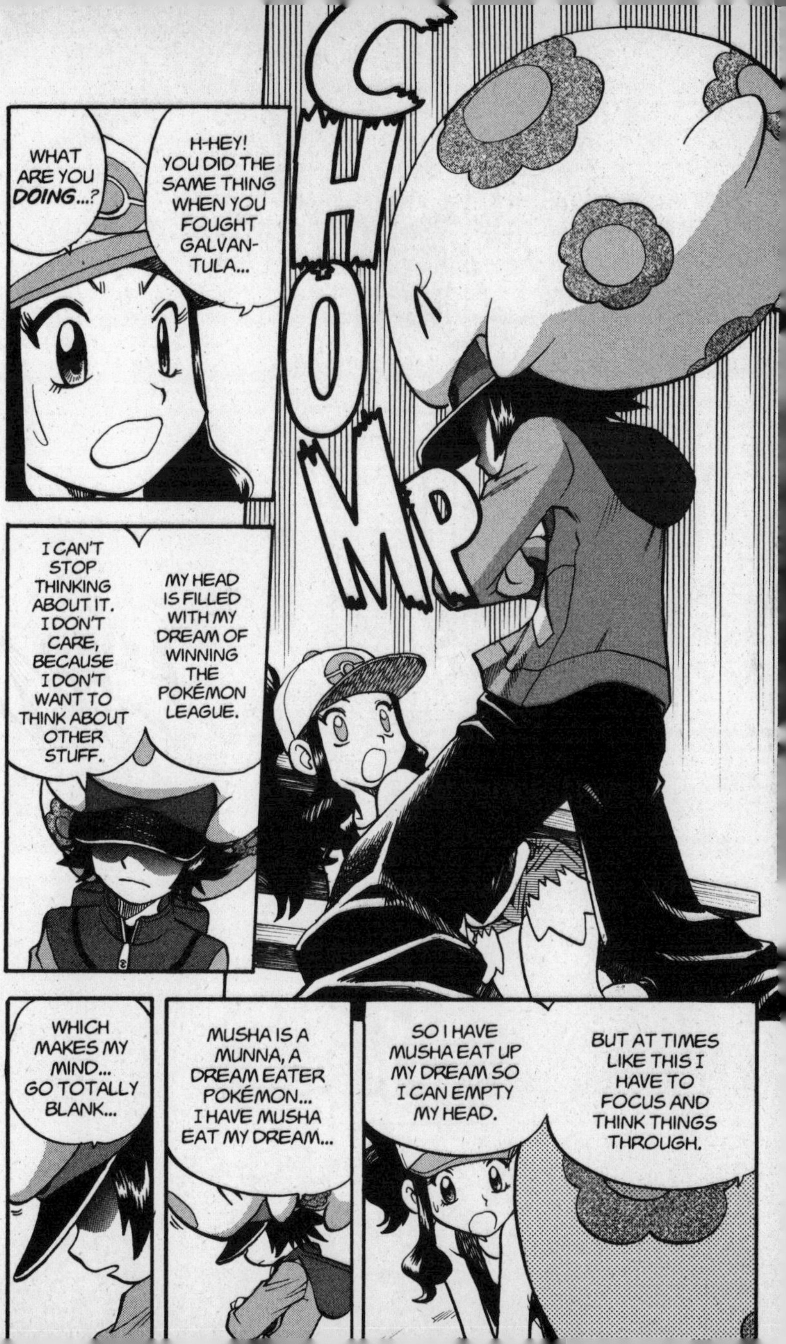
CHOMP
WHAT ARE YOU DOING...?
H-HEY! YOU DID THE SAME THING WHEN YOU FOUGHT GALVAN-TULA...
I CAN'T STOP THINKING ABOUT IT. I DON'T CARE, BECAUSE I DON'T WANT TO THINK ABOUT OTHER STUFF.
MY HEAD IS FILLED WITH MY DREAM OF WINNING THE POKÉMON LEAGUE.
WHICH MAKES MY MIND... GO TOTALLY BLANK...
MUSHA IS A MUNNA, A DREAM EATER POKÉMON... I HAVE MUSHA EAT MY DREAM...
SO I HAVE MUSHA EAT UP MY DREAM SO I CAN EMPTY MY HEAD.
BUT AT TIMES LIKE THIS I HAVE TO FOCUS AND THINK THINGS THROUGH.

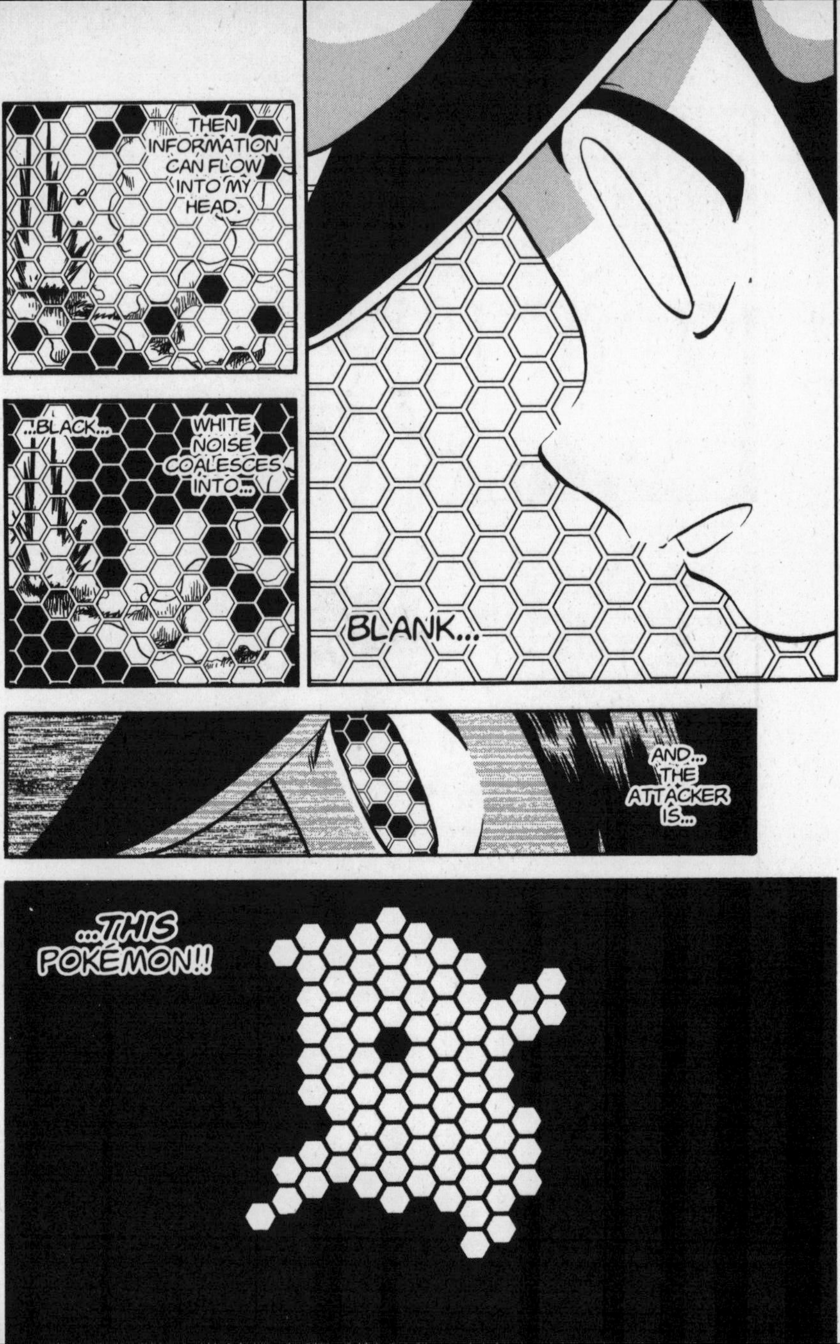

THEN INFORMATION CAN FLOW INTO MY HEAD.
BLANK...
...BLACK...
WHITE NOISE COALESCES INTO...
AND... THE ATTACKER IS...
...THIS POKÉMON!!

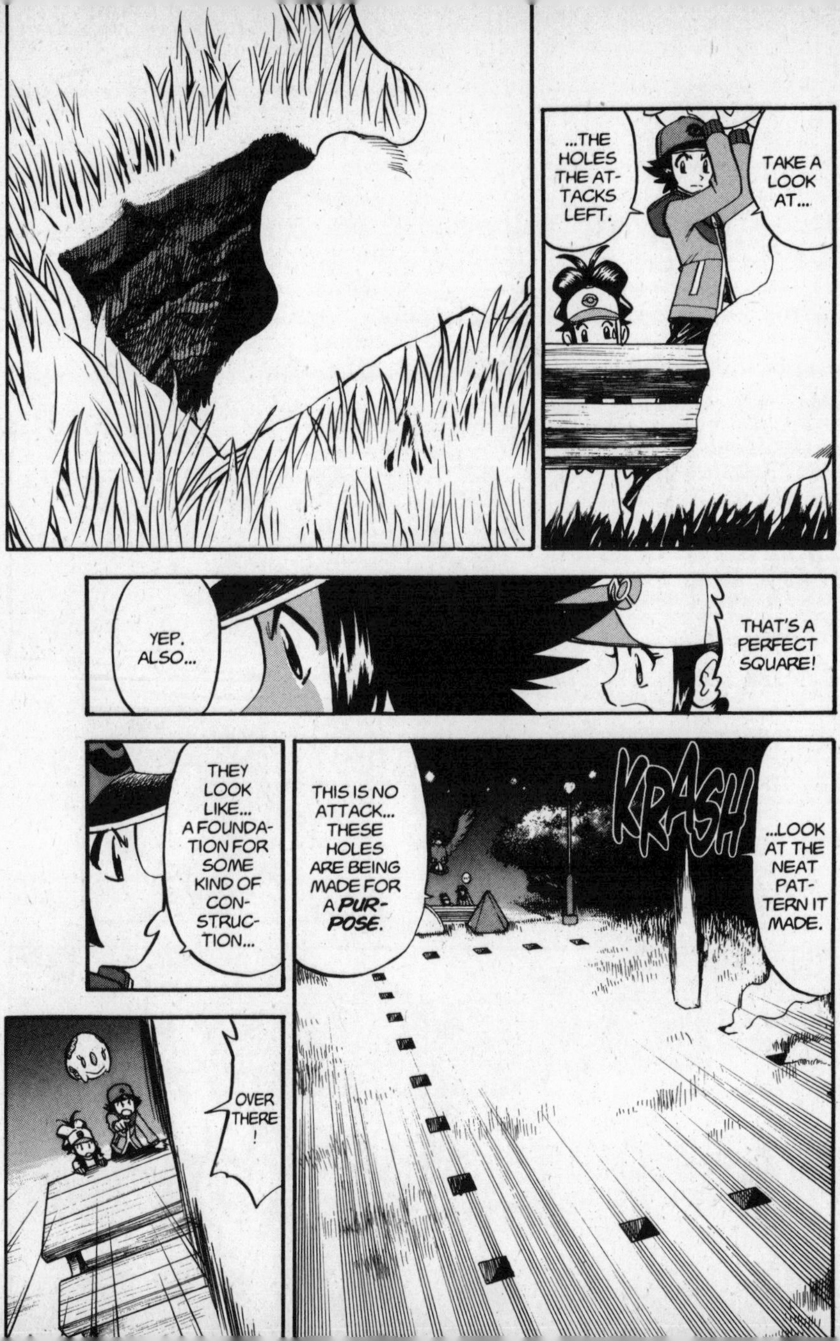
TAKE A LOOK AT...
...THE HOLES THE ATTACKS LEFT.
THAT'S A PERFECT SQUARE!
YEP. ALSO...
...LOOK AT THE NEAT PATTERN IT MADE.
KRASH
THIS IS NO ATTACK... THESE HOLES ARE BEING MADE FOR A PURPOSE.
THEY LOOK LIKE... A FOUNDATION FOR SOME KIND OF CONSTRUCTION...
OVER THERE!

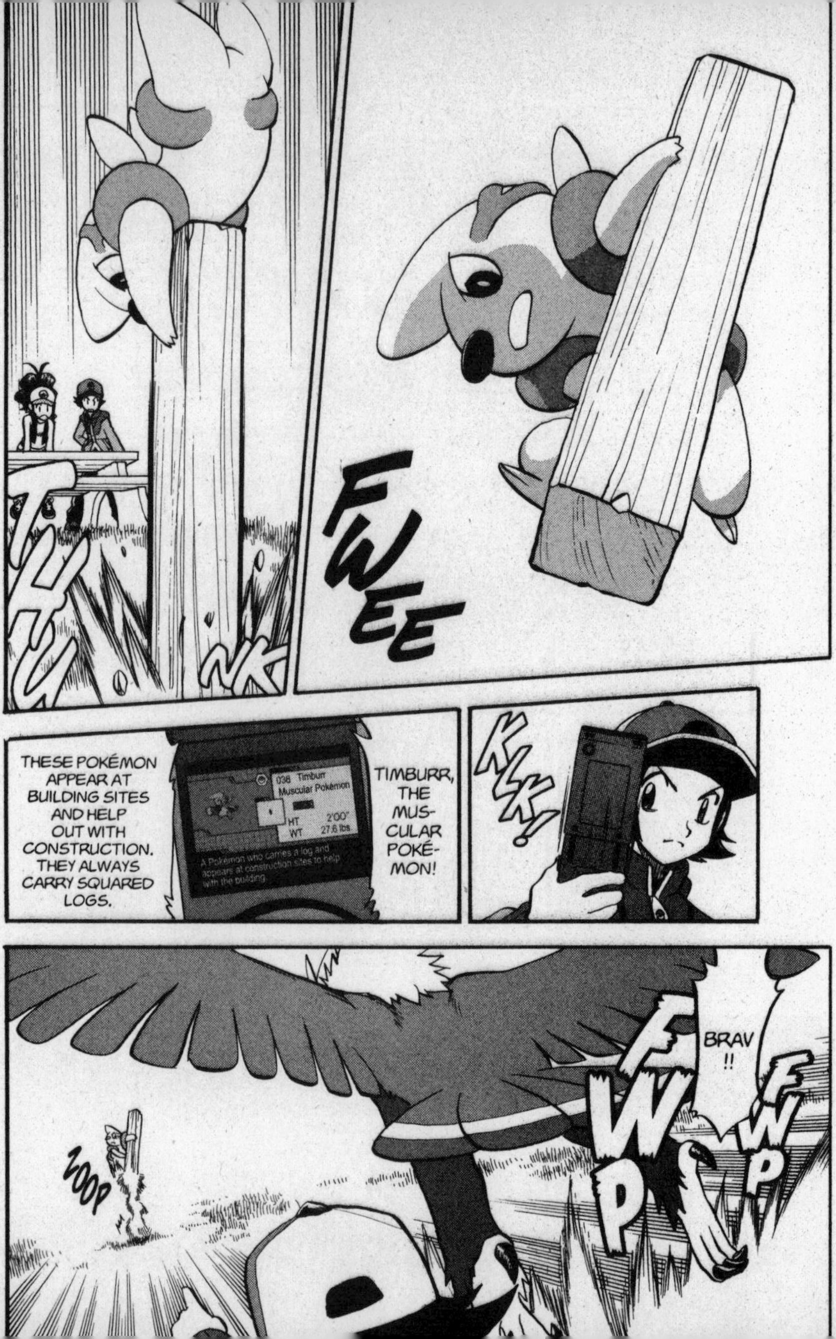

THU
NK
FWEEE
THESE POKÉMON APPEAR AT BUILDING SITES AND HELP OUT WITH CONSTRUCTION. THEY ALWAYS CARRY SQUARED LOGS.
038 Timburr
Muscular Pokémon
HT 2'00"
WT 27.6 lbs
A Pokémon who carries a log and appears at construction sites to help with the building.
TIMBURR, THE MUS-CULAR POKÉ-MON!
KLIK!
BRAV!!
FWP
FWP
ZOOP

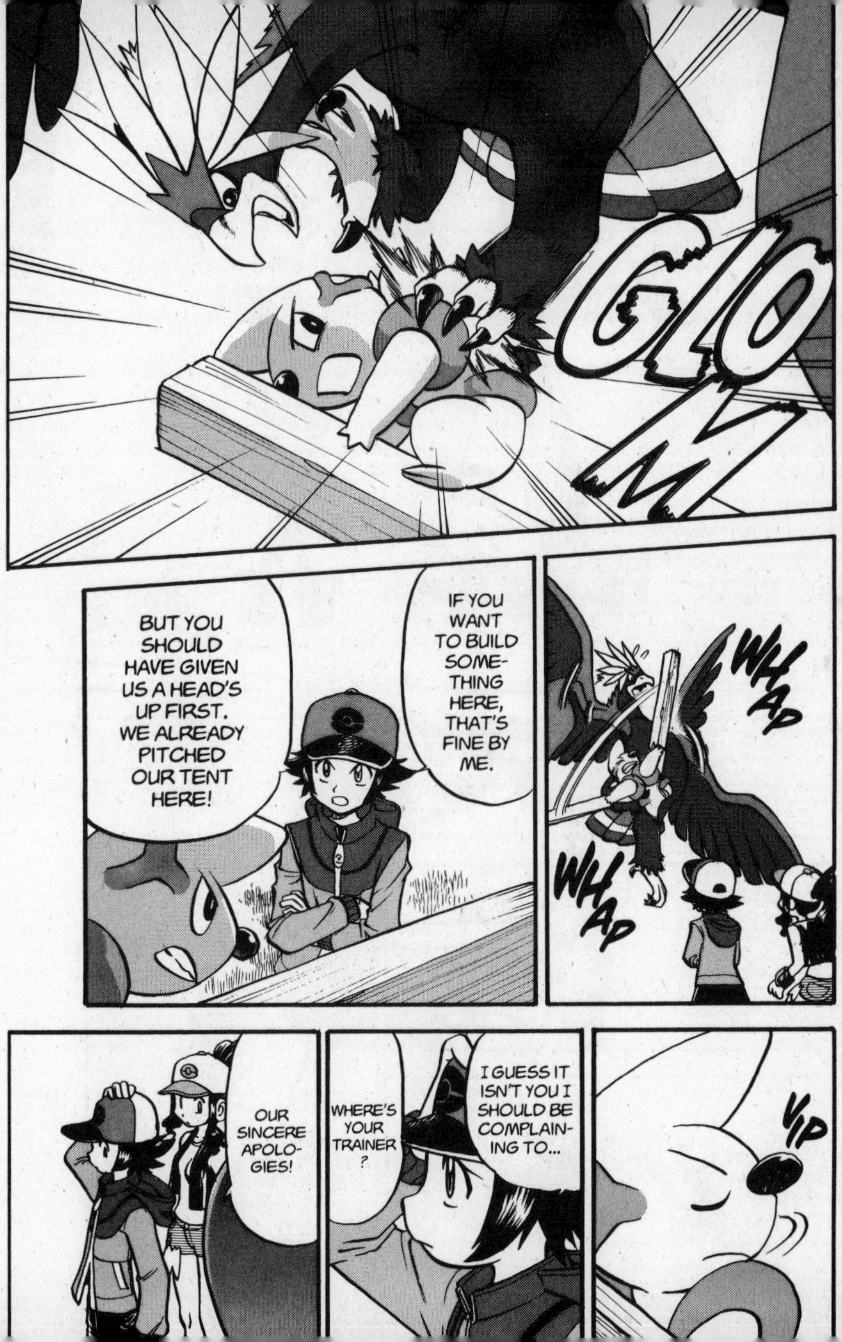
GLOOM
IF YOU WANT TO BUILD SOME-THING HERE, THAT'S FINE BY ME.
BUT YOU SHOULD HAVE GIVEN US A HEAD'S UP FIRST. WE ALREADY PITCHED OUR TENT HERE!
WHAP
WHAP
OUR SINCERE APOLO-GIES!
WHERE'S YOUR TRAINER ?
I GUESS IT ISN'T YOU I SHOULD BE COMPLAIN-ING TO...
YIP

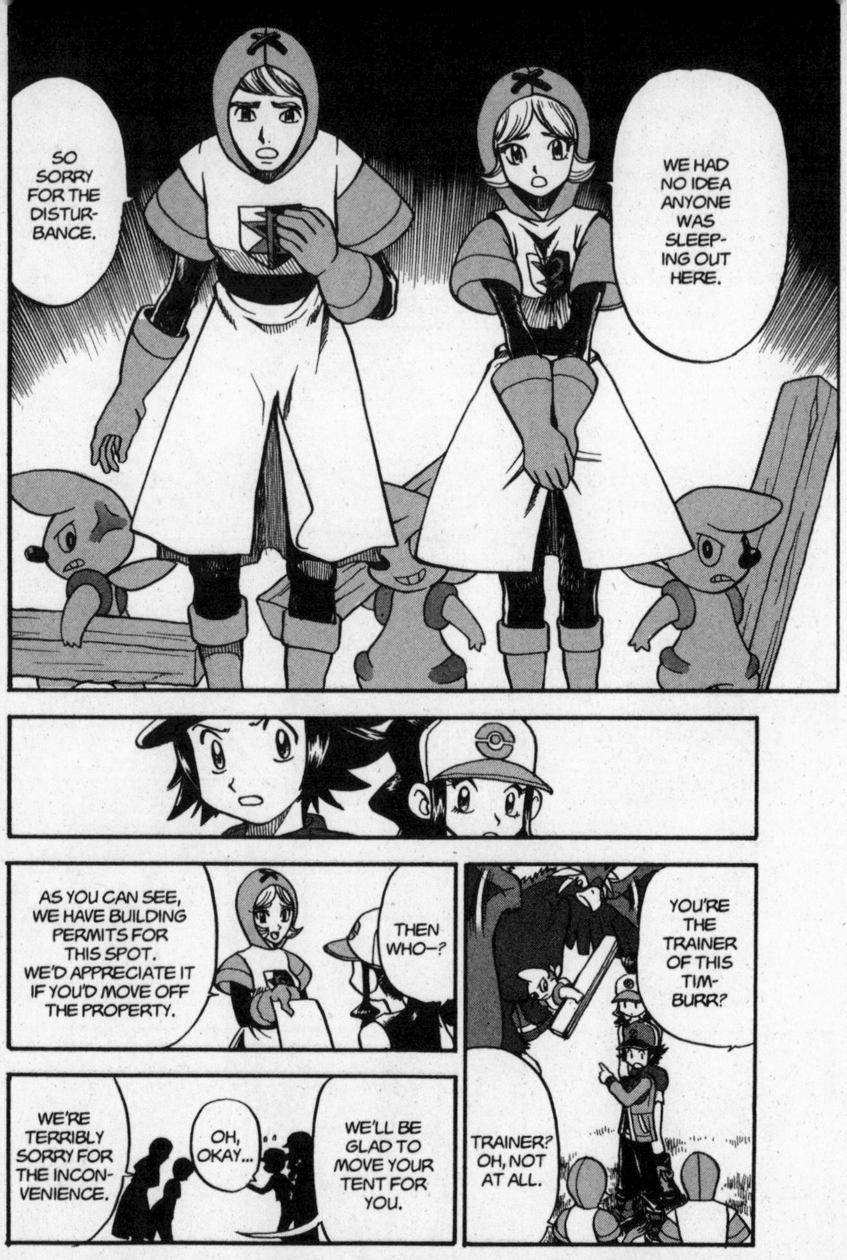
SO SORRY FOR THE DISTURBANCE.
WE HAD NO IDEA ANYONE WAS SLEEPING OUT HERE.
AS YOU CAN SEE, WE HAVE BUILDING PERMITS FOR THIS SPOT. WE'D APPRECIATE IT IF YOU'D MOVE OFF THE PROPERTY.
THEN WHO-?
YOU'RE THE TRAINER OF THIS TIMBURR?
WE'RE TERRIBLY SORRY FOR THE INCONVENIENCE.
OH, OKAY...
WE'LL BE GLAD TO MOVE YOUR TENT FOR YOU.
TRAINER? OH, NOT AT ALL.

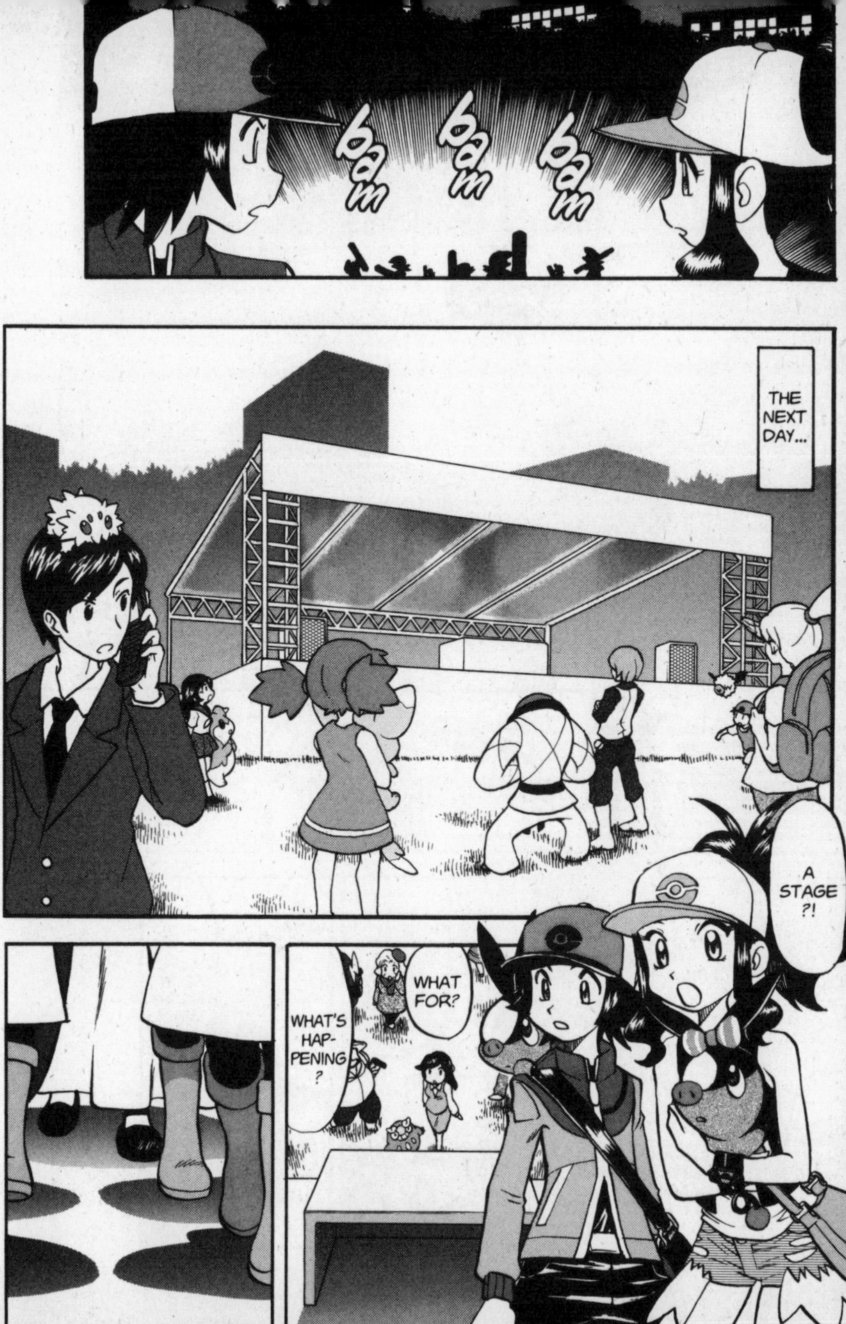
bam bam bam
THE NEXT DAY...
A STAGE ?!
WHAT FOR?
WHAT'S HAP- PENING ?

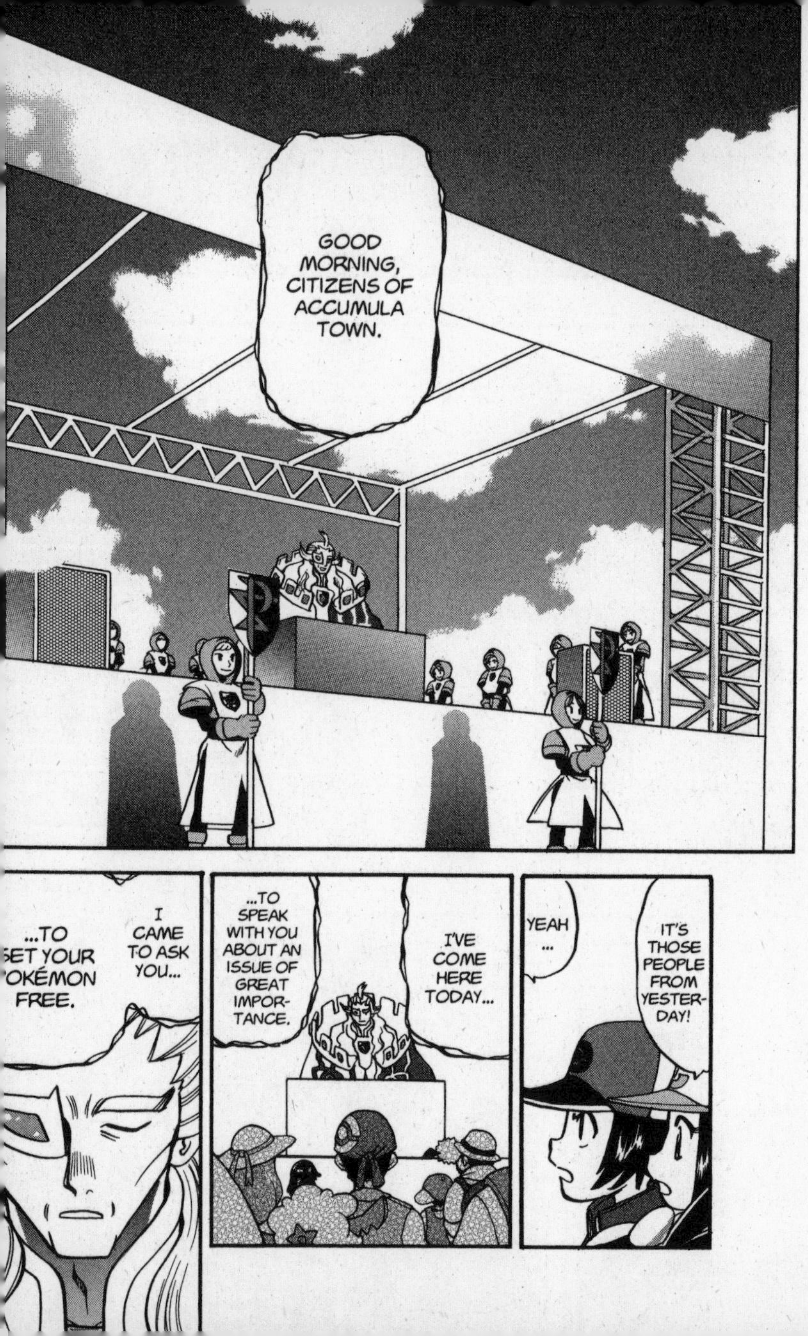
GOOD MORNING, CITIZENS OF ACCUMULA TOWN.
IT'S THOSE PEOPLE FROM YESTER-DAY!
YEAH ...
I'VE COME HERE TODAY...
...TO SPEAK WITH YOU ABOUT AN ISSUE OF GREAT IMPOR-TANCE.
I CAME TO ASK YOU...
...TO SET YOUR OKÉMON FREE.

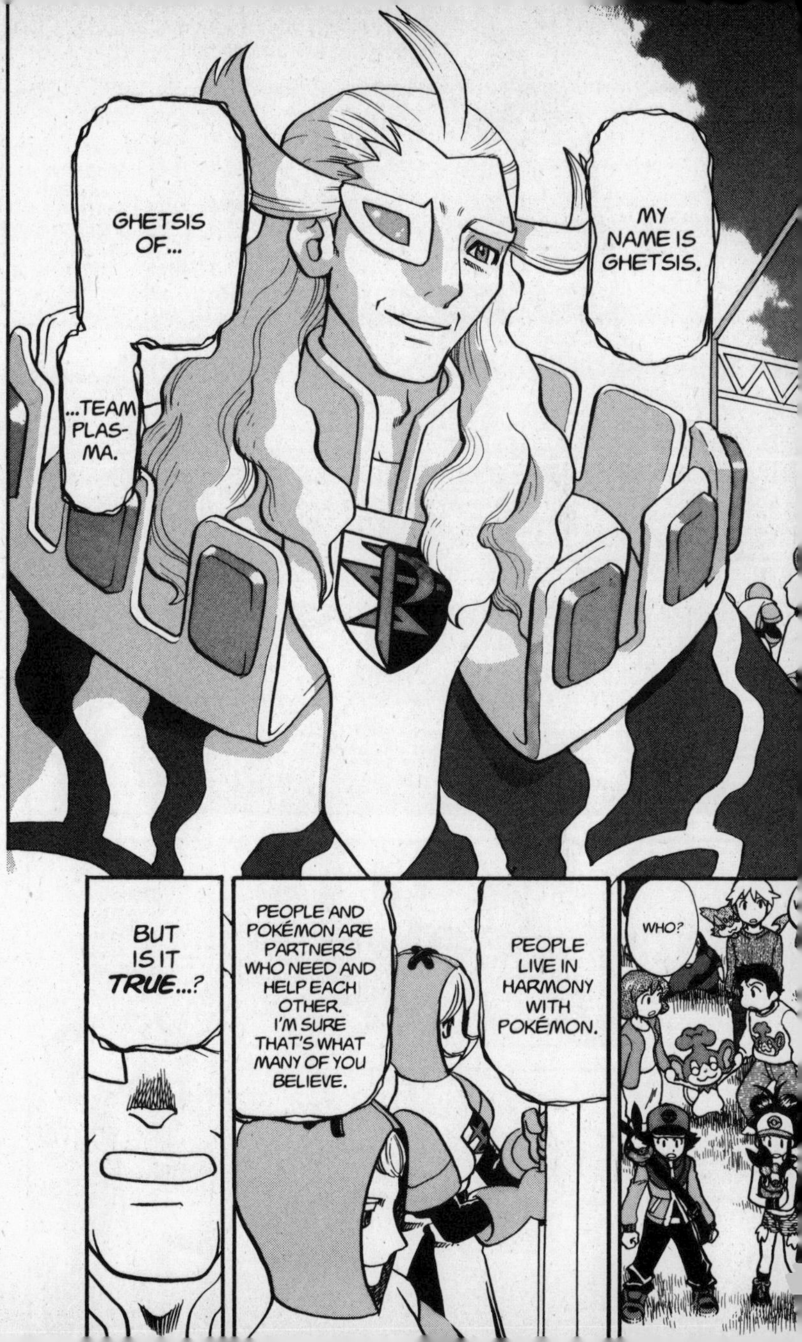
MY NAME IS GHETSIS.
GHETSIS OF...
...TEAM PLAS-MA.
WHO?
PEOPLE LIVE IN HARMONY WITH POKÉMON.
PEOPLE AND POKÉMON ARE PARTNERS WHO NEED AND HELP EACH OTHER. I'M SURE THAT'S WHAT MANY OF YOU BELIEVE.
BUT IS IT *TRUE*...?

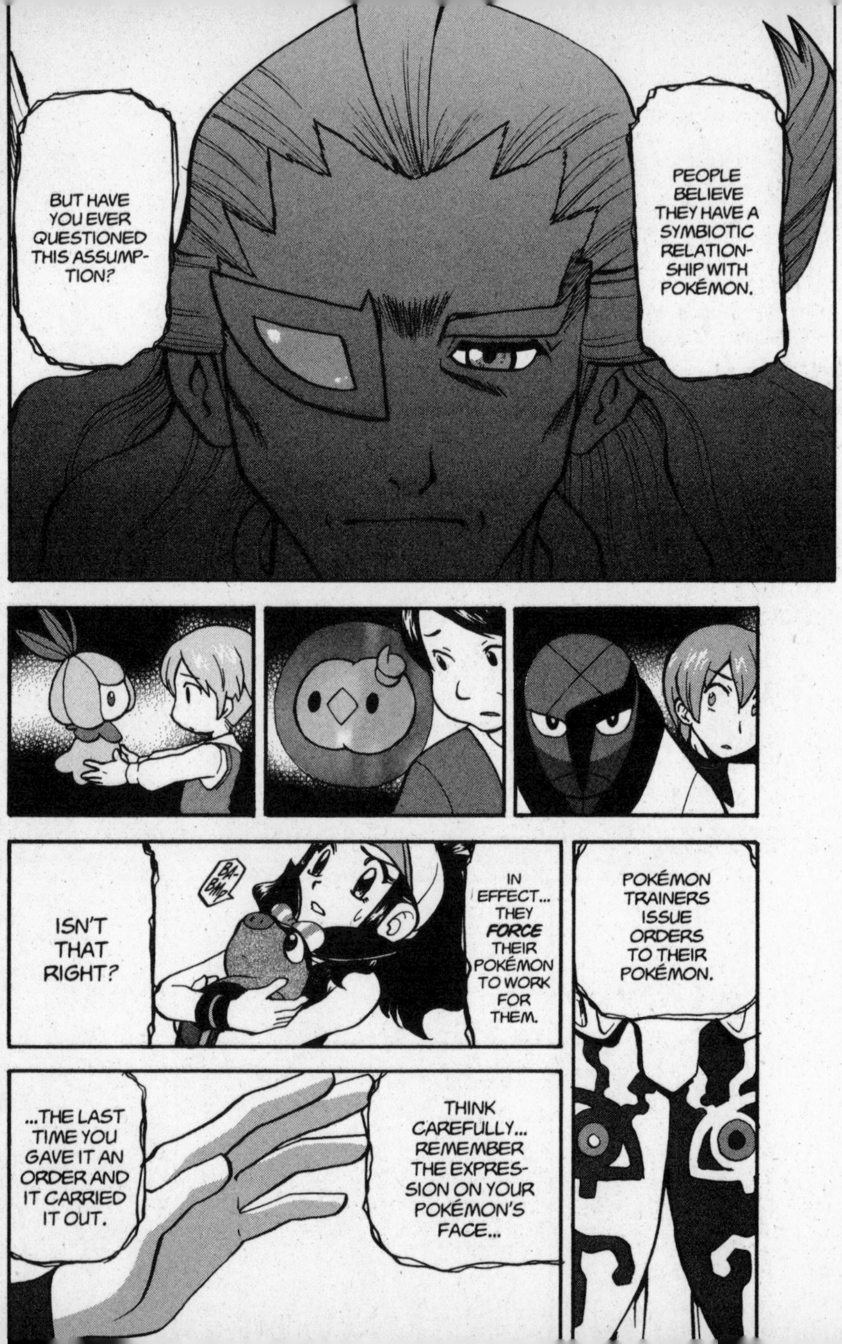

PEOPLE BELIEVE THEY HAVE A SYMBIOTIC RELATION-SHIP WITH POKÉMON.
BUT HAVE YOU EVER QUESTIONED THIS ASSUMP-TION?
POKÉMON TRAINERS ISSUE ORDERS TO THEIR POKÉMON.
IN EFFECT... THEY **FORCE** THEIR POKÉMON TO WORK FOR THEM.
BA-BMP
ISN'T THAT RIGHT?
THINK CAREFULLY... REMEMBER THE EXPRES-SION ON YOUR POKÉMON'S FACE...
...THE LAST TIME YOU GAVE IT AN ORDER AND IT CARRIED IT OUT.

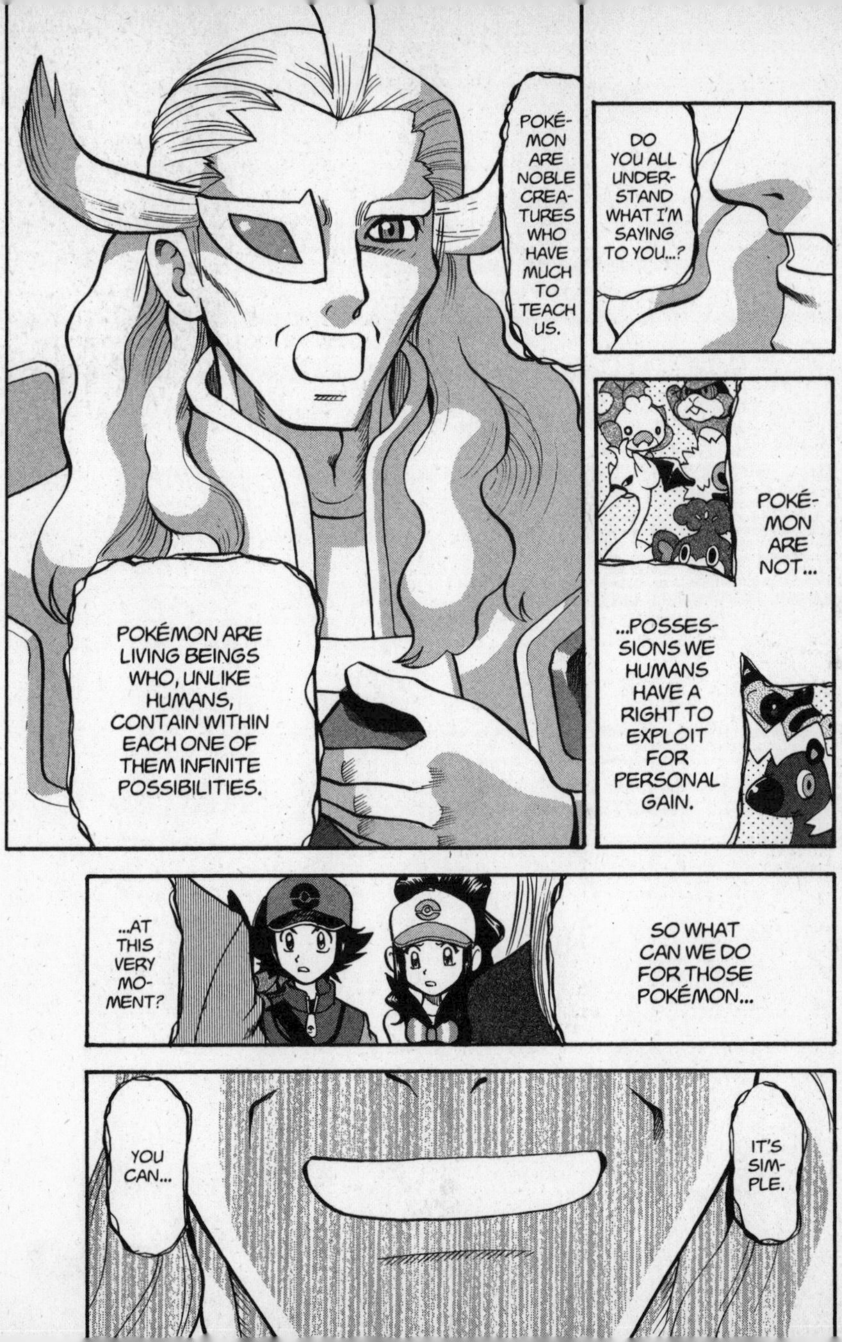
POKÉMON ARE NOBLE CREATURES WHO HAVE MUCH TO TEACH US.
DO YOU ALL UNDERSTAND WHAT I'M SAYING TO YOU...?
POKÉMON ARE LIVING BEINGS WHO, UNLIKE HUMANS, CONTAIN WITHIN EACH ONE OF THEM INFINITE POSSIBILITIES.
POKÉMON ARE NOT...
...POSSESSIONS WE HUMANS HAVE A RIGHT TO EXPLOIT FOR PERSONAL GAIN.
SO WHAT CAN WE DO FOR THOSE POKÉMON...
...AT THIS VERY MOMENT?
IT'S SIMPLE.
YOU CAN...

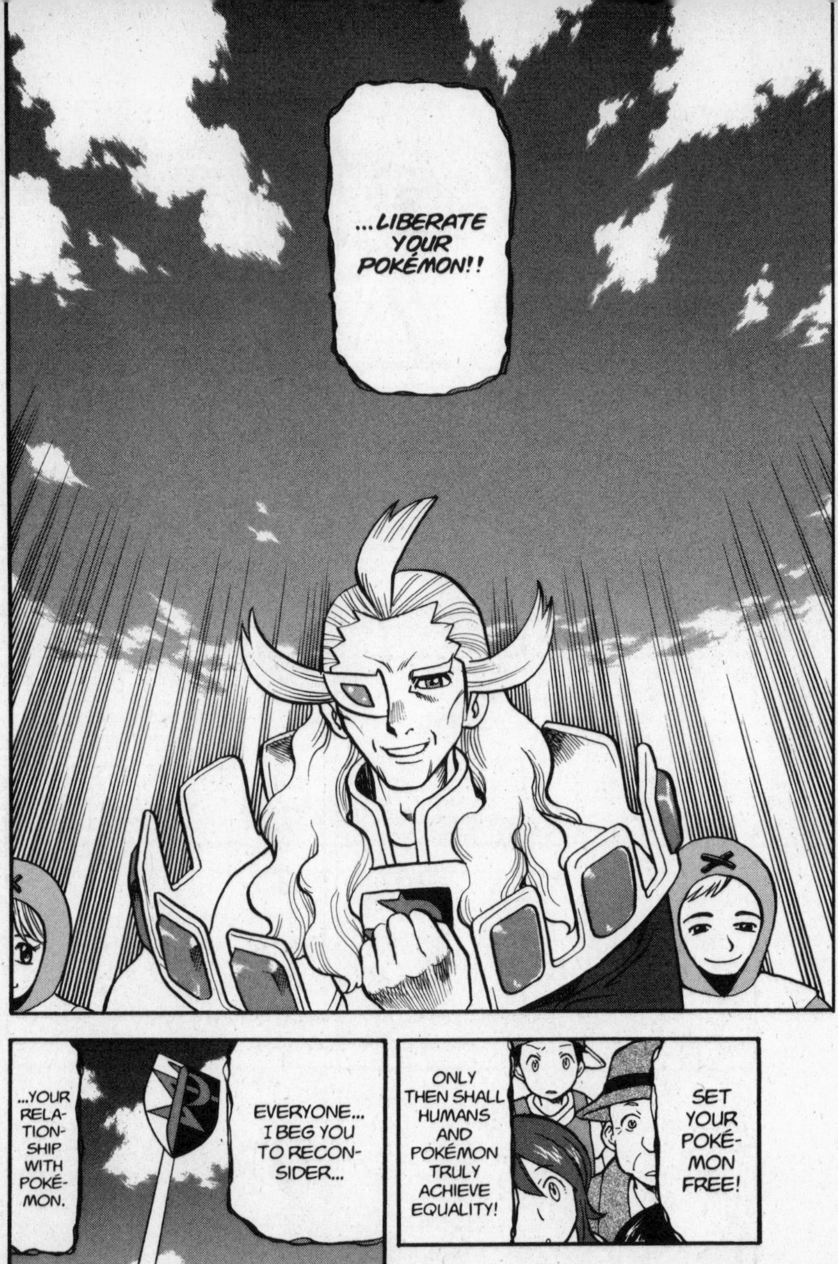
...LIBERATE YOUR POKÉMON!!
EVERYONE... I BEG YOU TO RECONSIDER...
...YOUR RELATIONSHIP WITH POKÉMON.
SET YOUR POKÉMON FREE!
ONLY THEN SHALL HUMANS AND POKÉMON TRULY ACHIEVE EQUALITY!

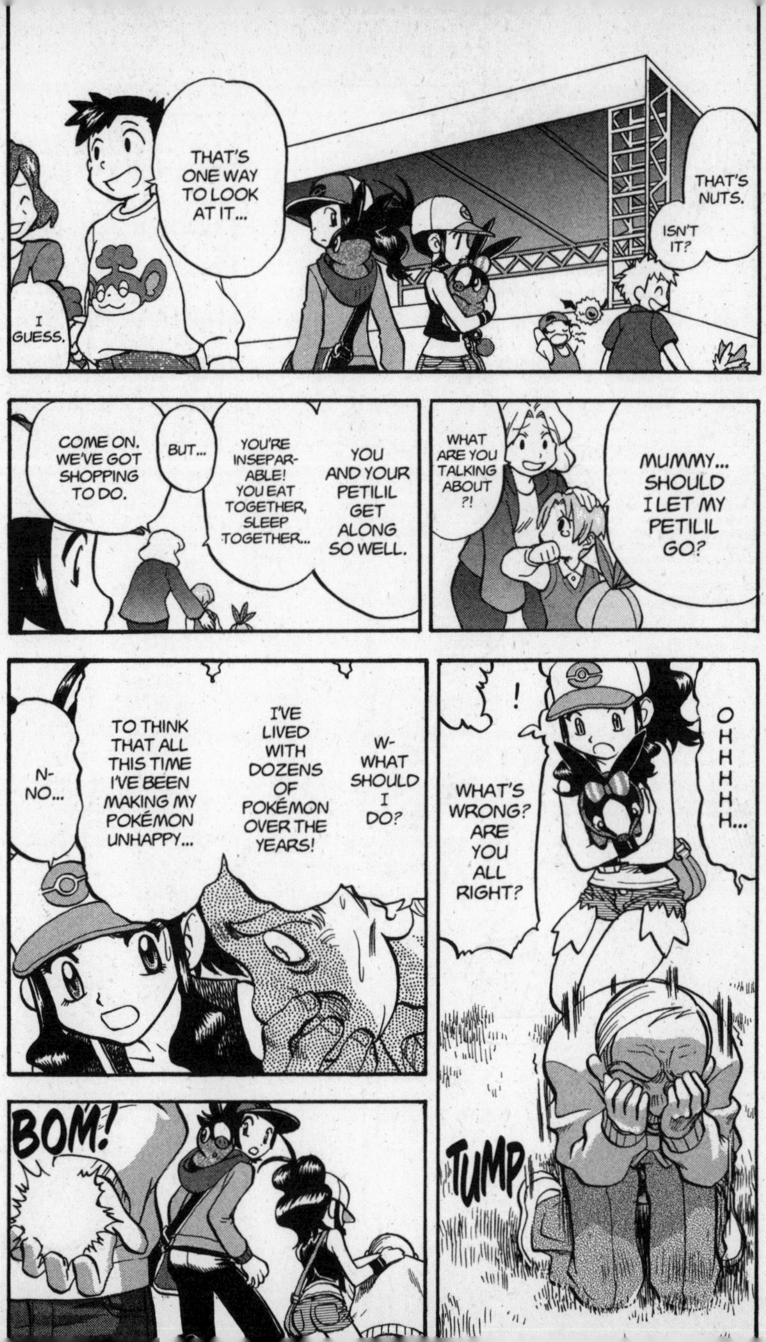
THAT'S ONE WAY TO LOOK AT IT...
I GUESS.
THAT'S NUTS.
ISN'T IT?
COME ON. WE'VE GOT SHOPPING TO DO.
BUT...
YOU'RE INSEPARABLE! YOU EAT TOGETHER, SLEEP TOGETHER...
YOU AND YOUR PETILIL GET ALONG SO WELL.
WHAT ARE YOU TALKING ABOUT?!
MUMMY... SHOULD I LET MY PETILIL GO?
N-NO...
TO THINK THAT ALL THIS TIME I'VE BEEN MAKING MY POKÉMON UNHAPPY...
I'VE LIVED WITH DOZENS OF POKÉMON OVER THE YEARS!
W-WHAT SHOULD I DO?
!
WHAT'S WRONG? ARE YOU ALL RIGHT?
OHHHHH...
BOM!
TUMP

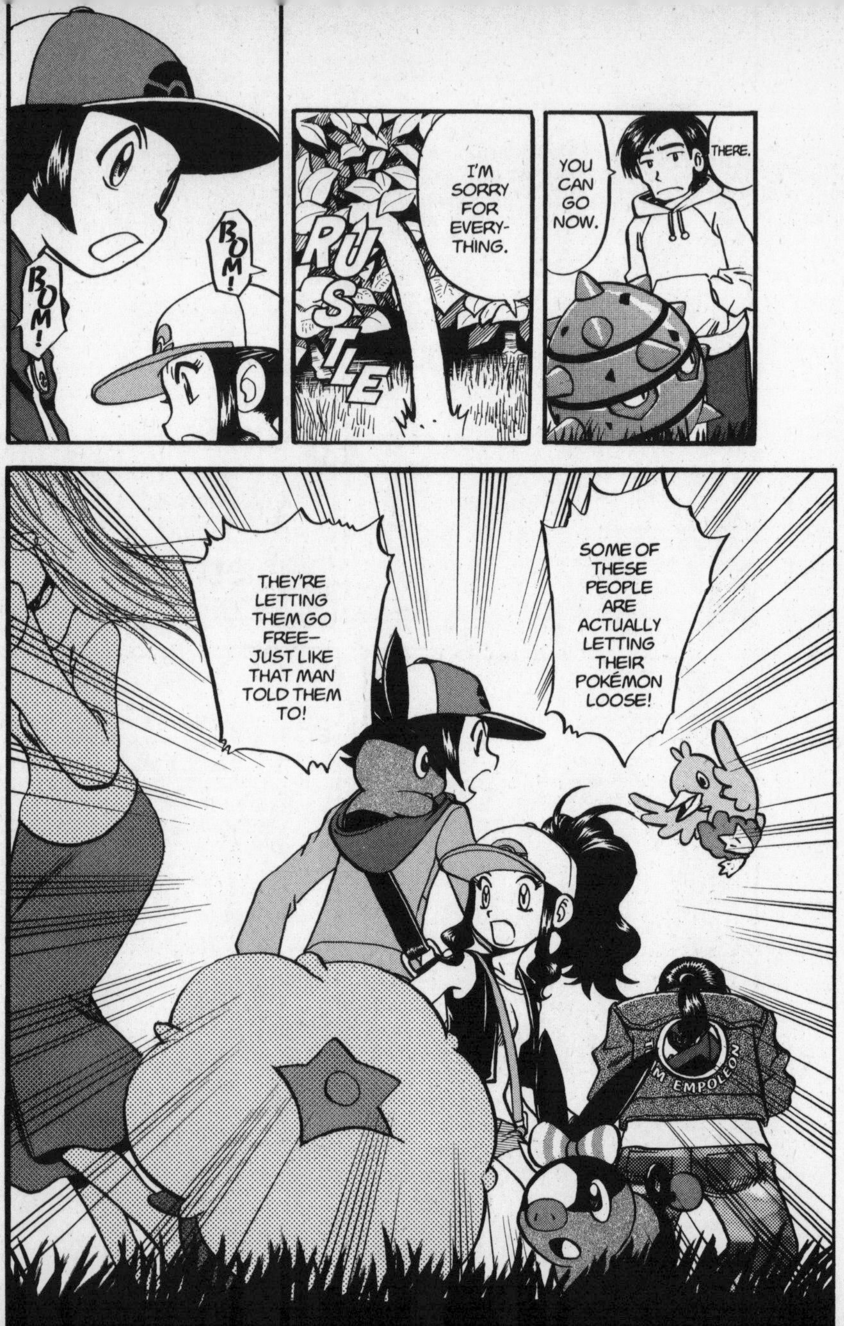

ROM! ROM!
ROM!
I'M SORRY FOR EVERY-THING.
RUSTLE
YOU CAN GO NOW.
THERE.
SOME OF THESE PEOPLE ARE ACTUALLY LETTING THEIR POKÉMON LOOSE!
THEY'RE LETTING THEM GO FREE—JUST LIKE THAT MAN TOLD THEM TO!
M EMPOLEON

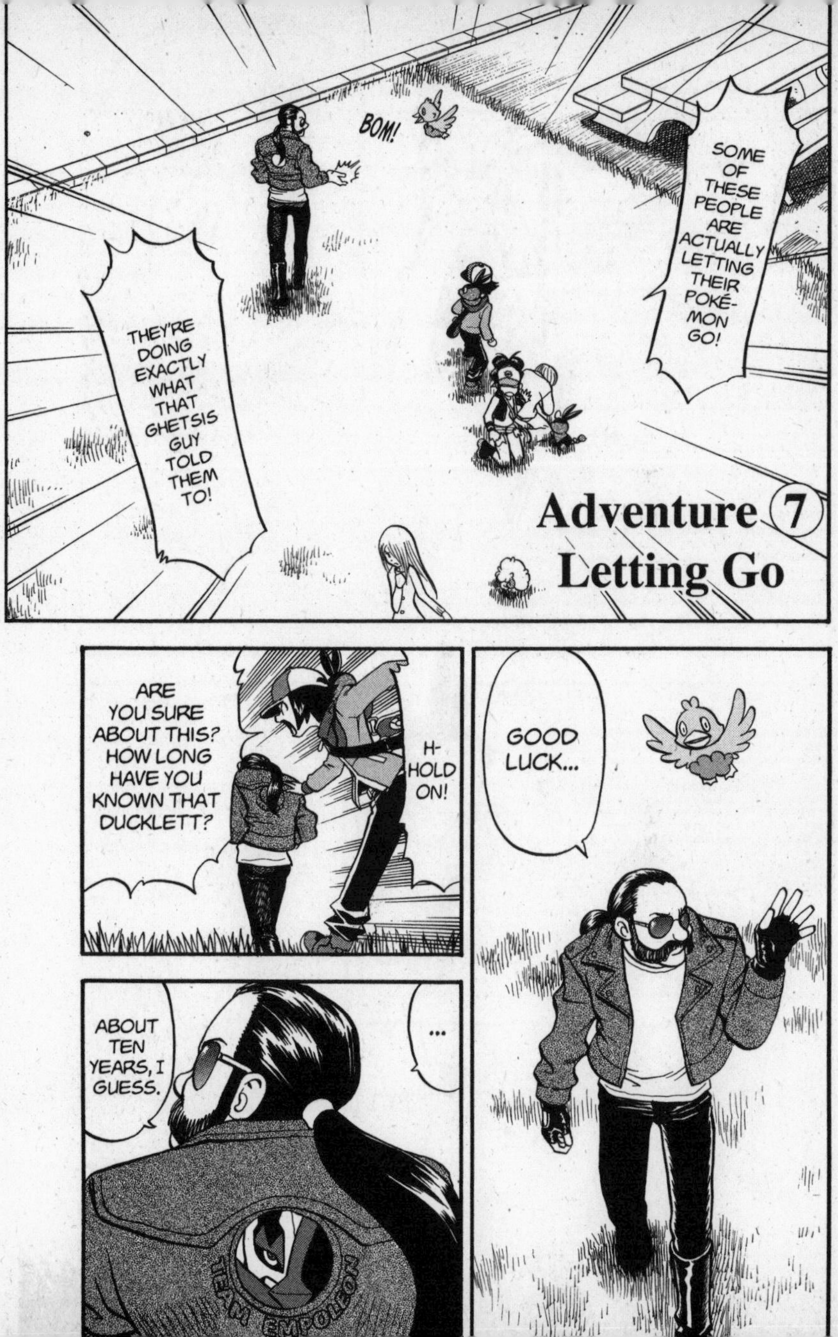

THEY'RE DOING EXACTLY WHAT THAT GHETSIS GUY TOLD THEM TO!
BOM!
SOME OF THESE PEOPLE ARE ACTUALLY LETTING THEIR POKÉMON GO!
Adventure 7
Letting Go
ARE YOU SURE ABOUT THIS? HOW LONG HAVE YOU KNOWN THAT DUCKLETT?
H-HOLD ON!
GOOD LUCK...
ABOUT TEN YEARS, I GUESS.
...

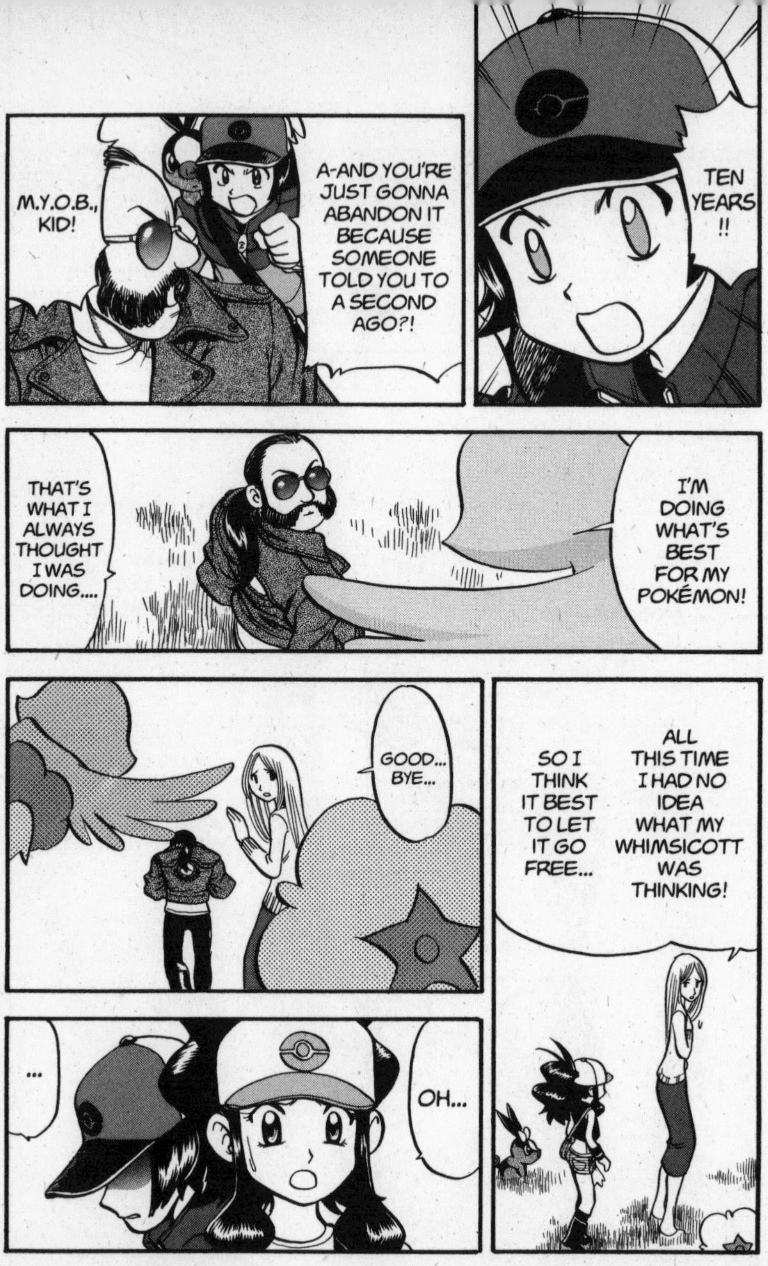
TEN YEARS !!
A-AND YOU'RE JUST GONNA ABANDON IT BECAUSE SOMEONE TOLD YOU TO A SECOND AGO?!
M.Y.O.B., KID!
I'M DOING WHAT'S BEST FOR MY POKÉMON!
THAT'S WHAT I ALWAYS THOUGHT I WAS DOING....
ALL THIS TIME I HAD NO IDEA WHAT MY WHIMSICOTT WAS THINKING!
SO I THINK IT BEST TO LET IT GO FREE...
GOOD... BYE...
OH...
...

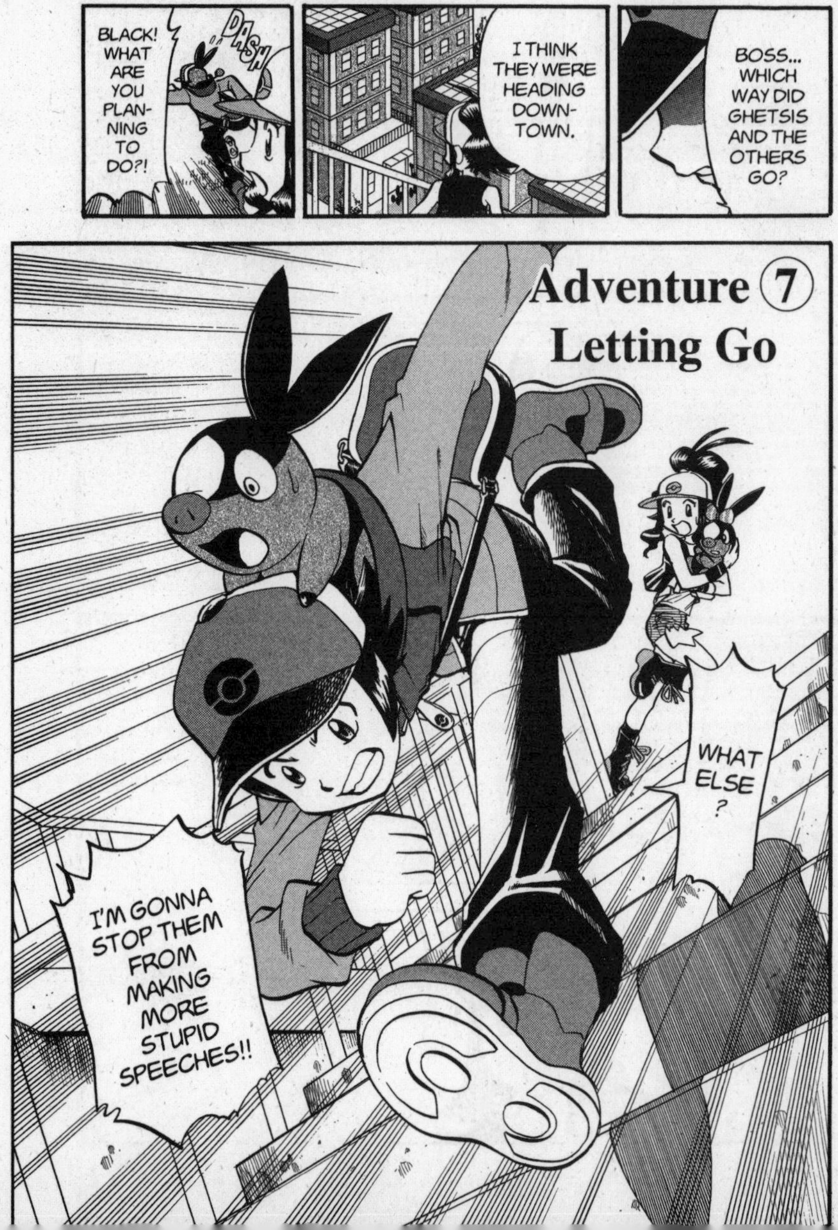
BOSS... WHICH WAY DID GHETSIS AND THE OTHERS GO?
I THINK THEY WERE HEADING DOWN-TOWN.
BLACK! WHAT ARE YOU PLAN-NING TO DO?!
DASH
Adventure 7 Letting Go
WHAT ELSE ?
I'M GONNA STOP THEM FROM MAKING MORE STUPID SPEECHES!!

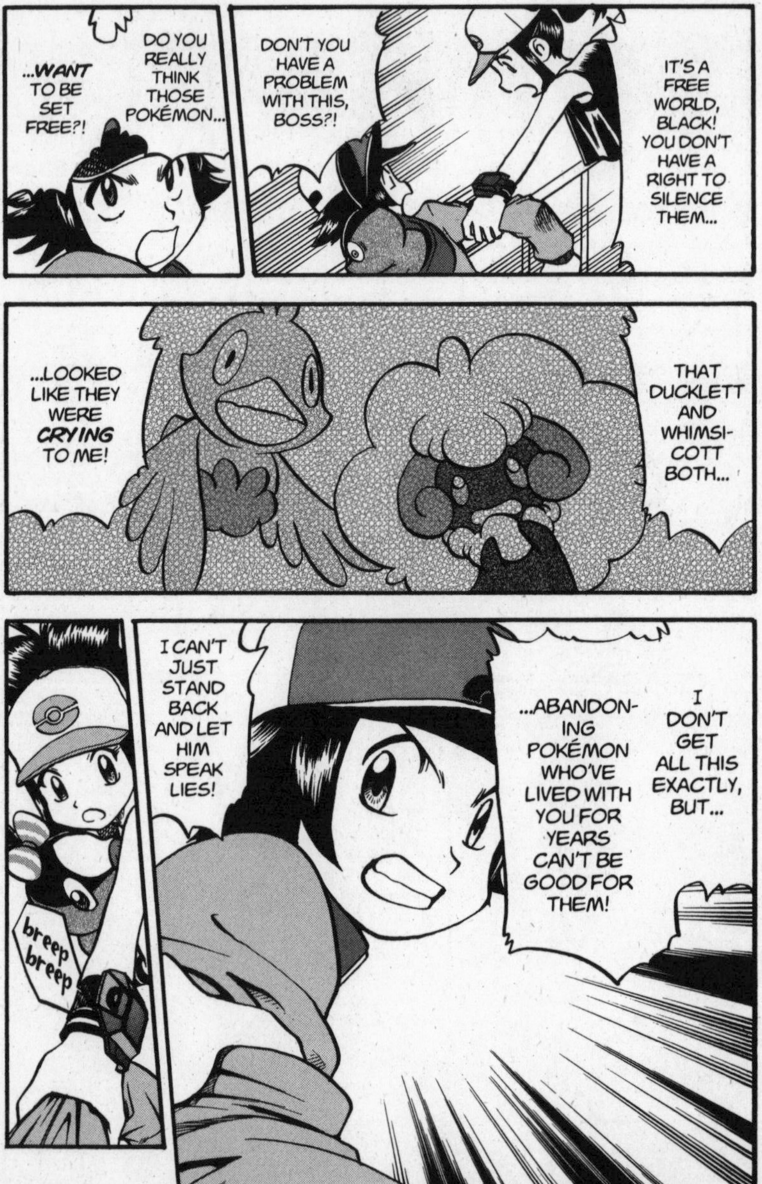
IT'S A FREE WORLD, BLACK! YOU DON'T HAVE A RIGHT TO SILENCE THEM...
DON'T YOU HAVE A PROBLEM WITH THIS, BOSS?!
DO YOU REALLY THINK THOSE POKÉMON...
...WANT TO BE SET FREE?!
THAT DUCKLETT AND WHIMSI-COTT BOTH...
...LOOKED LIKE THEY WERE CRYING TO ME!
I DON'T GET ALL THIS EXACTLY, BUT...
...ABANDON-ING POKÉMON WHO'VE LIVED WITH YOU FOR YEARS CAN'T BE GOOD FOR THEM!
I CAN'T JUST STAND BACK AND LET HIM SPEAK LIES!
breep breep

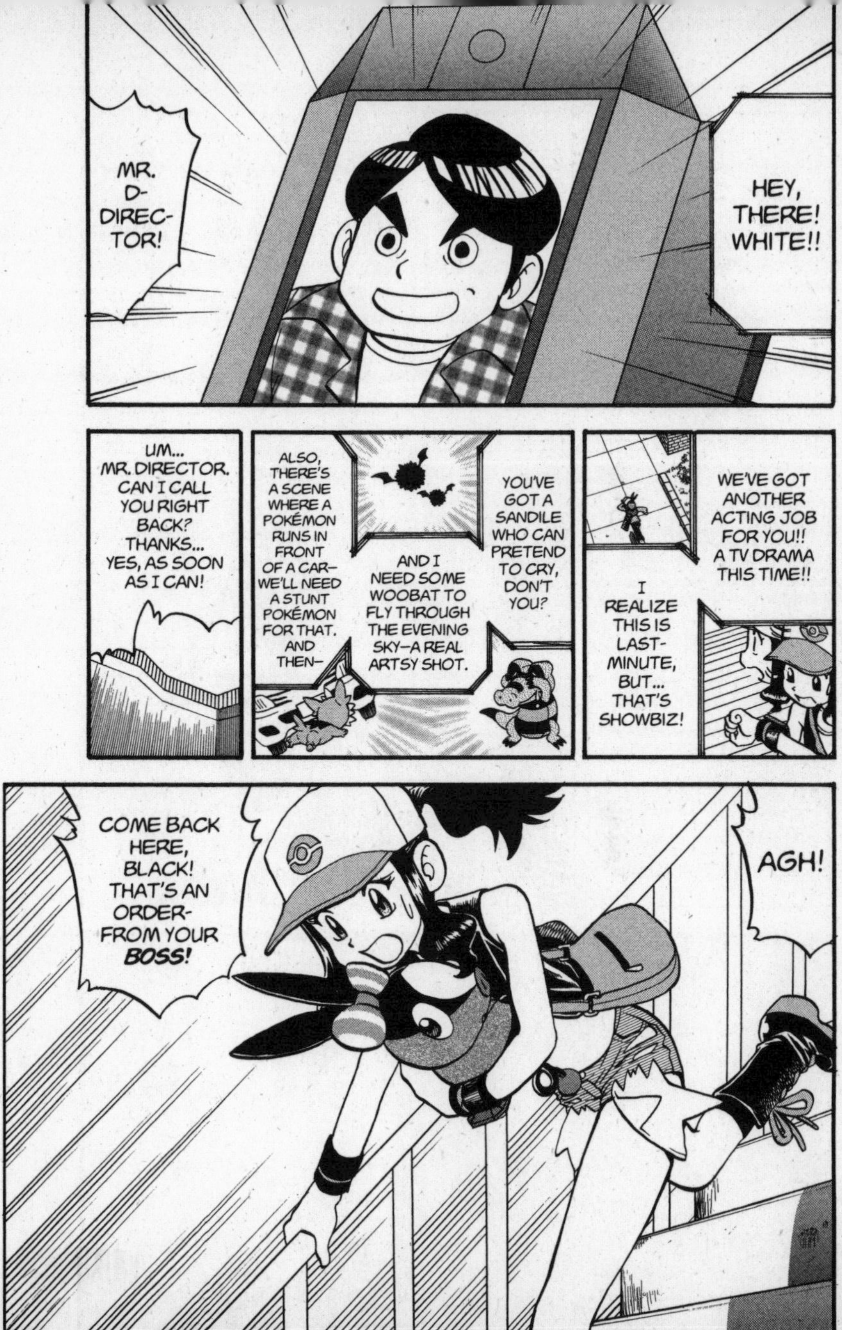
HEY, THERE! WHITE!!
MR. D-DIRECTOR!
WE'VE GOT ANOTHER ACTING JOB FOR YOU!! A TV DRAMA THIS TIME!!
I REALIZE THIS IS LAST-MINUTE, BUT... THAT'S SHOWBIZ!
YOU'VE GOT A SANDILE WHO CAN PRETEND TO CRY, DON'T YOU?
AND I NEED SOME WOOBAT TO FLY THROUGH THE EVENING SKY—A REAL ARTSY SHOT.
ALSO, THERE'S A SCENE WHERE A POKÉMON RUNS IN FRONT OF A CAR—WE'LL NEED A STUNT POKÉMON FOR THAT. AND THEN—
UM... MR. DIRECTOR. CAN I CALL YOU RIGHT BACK? THANKS... YES, AS SOON AS I CAN!
AGH!
COME BACK HERE, BLACK! THAT'S AN ORDER-FROM YOUR BOSS!

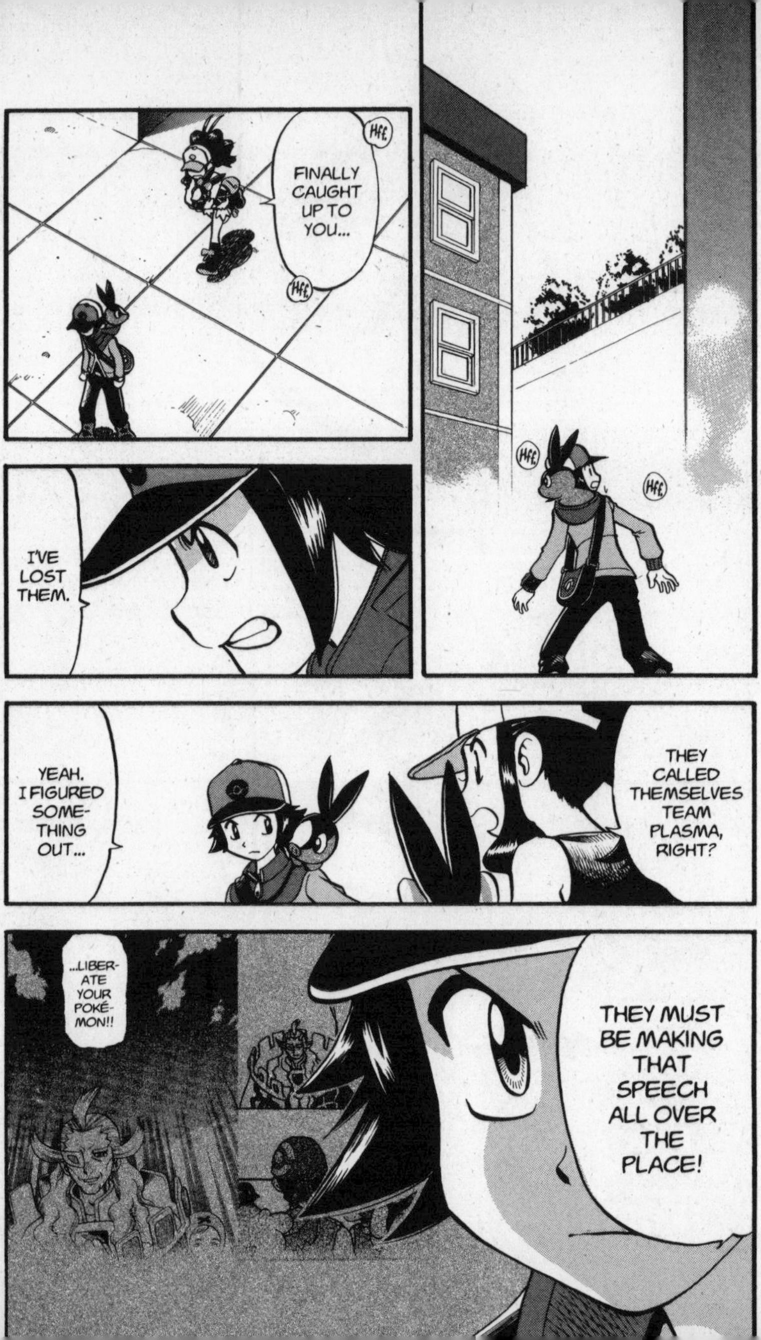
HFF.
FINALLY CAUGHT UP TO YOU...
HFF.
HFF.
HFF.
I'VE LOST THEM.
YEAH. I FIGURED SOME-THING OUT...
THEY CALLED THEMSELVES TEAM PLASMA, RIGHT?
...LIBER-ATE YOUR POKÉ-MON!!
THEY MUST BE MAKING THAT SPEECH ALL OVER THE PLACE!

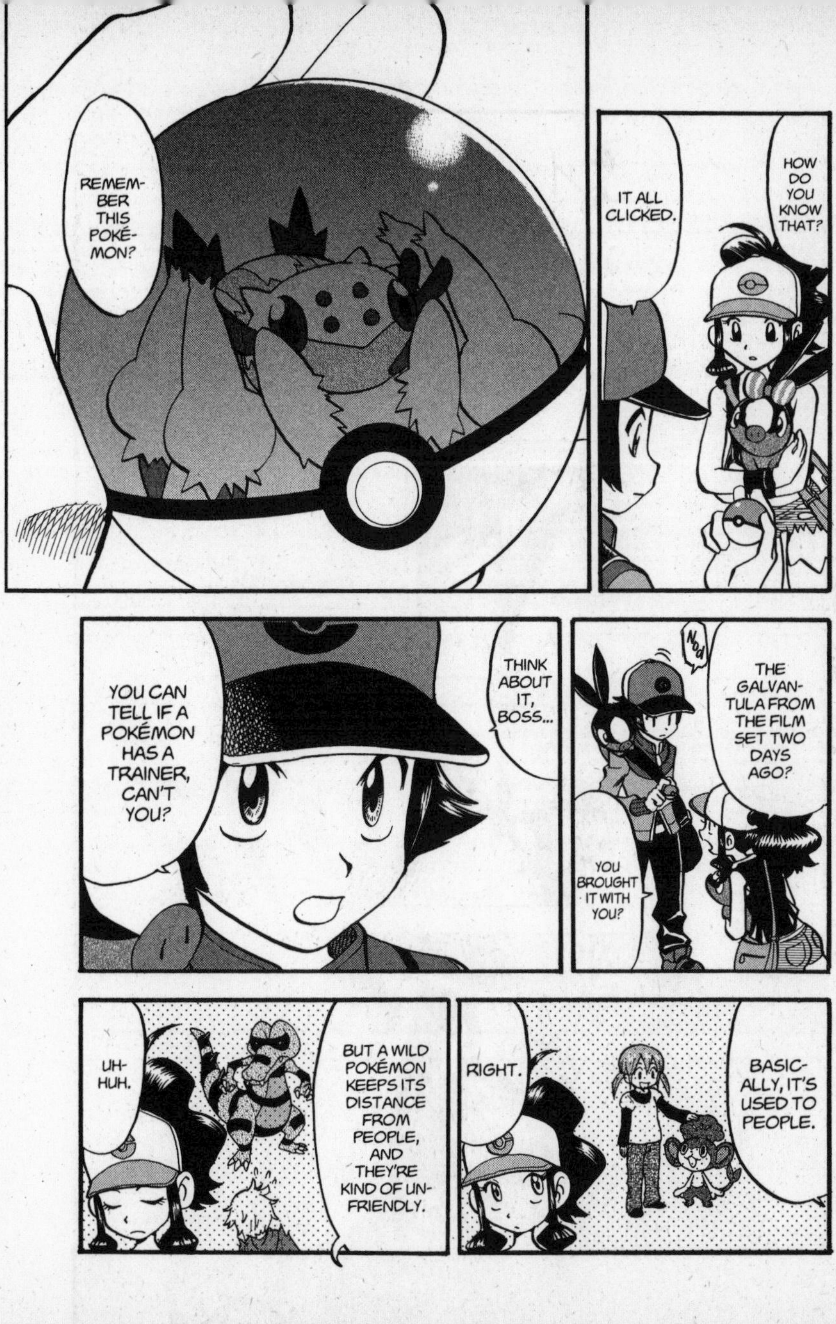
HOW DO YOU KNOW THAT?
IT ALL CLICKED.
REMEMBER THIS POKÉMON?
THE GALVANTULA FROM THE FILM SET TWO DAYS AGO?
Nod
YOU BROUGHT IT WITH YOU?
THINK ABOUT IT, BOSS...
YOU CAN TELL IF A POKÉMON HAS A TRAINER, CAN'T YOU?
BASICALLY, IT'S USED TO PEOPLE.
RIGHT.
BUT A WILD POKÉMON KEEPS ITS DISTANCE FROM PEOPLE, AND THEY'RE KIND OF UNFRIENDLY.
UH-HUH.

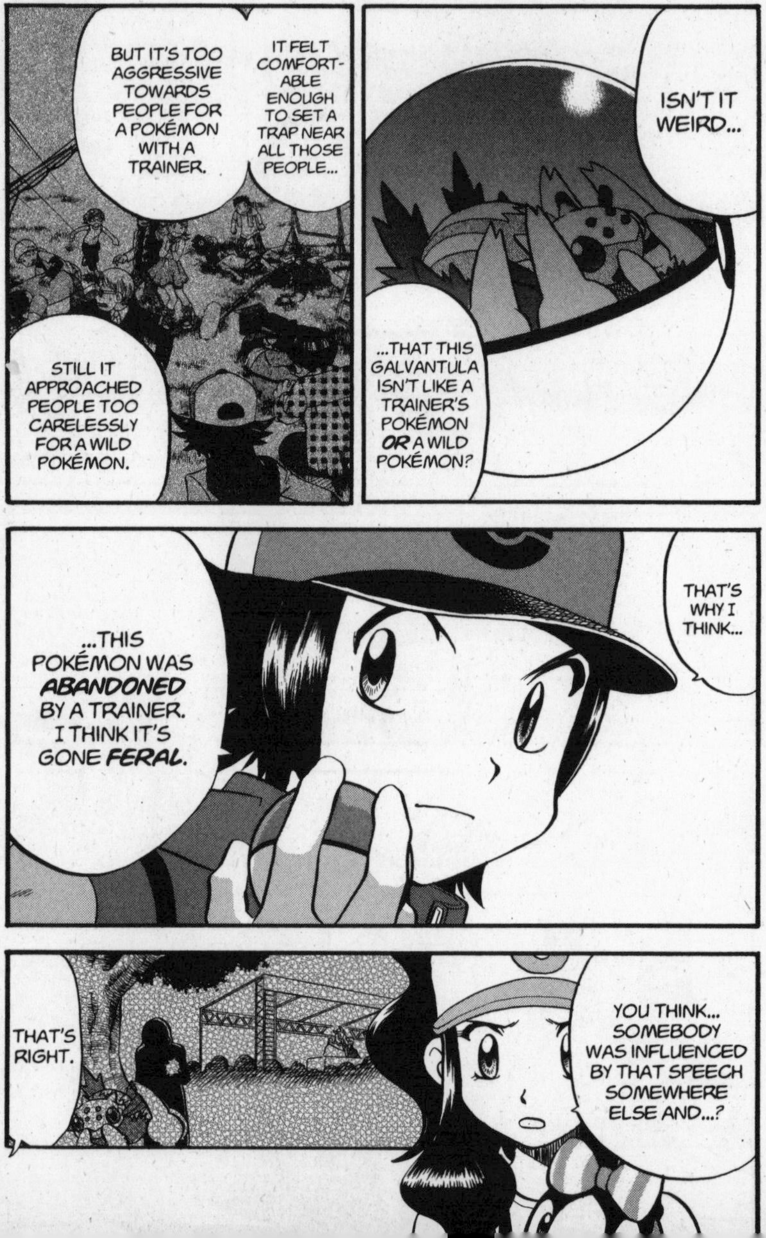
ISN'T IT WEIRD...
...THAT THIS GALVANTULA ISN'T LIKE A TRAINER'S POKÉMON OR A WILD POKÉMON?
IT FELT COMFORT-ABLE ENOUGH TO SET A TRAP NEAR ALL THOSE PEOPLE...
BUT IT'S TOO AGGRESSIVE TOWARDS PEOPLE FOR A POKÉMON WITH A TRAINER.
STILL IT APPROACHED PEOPLE TOO CARELESSLY FOR A WILD POKÉMON.
THAT'S WHY I THINK...
...THIS POKÉMON WAS ABANDONED BY A TRAINER. I THINK IT'S GONE FERAL.
YOU THINK... SOMEBODY WAS INFLUENCED BY THAT SPEECH SOMEWHERE ELSE AND...?
THAT'S RIGHT.

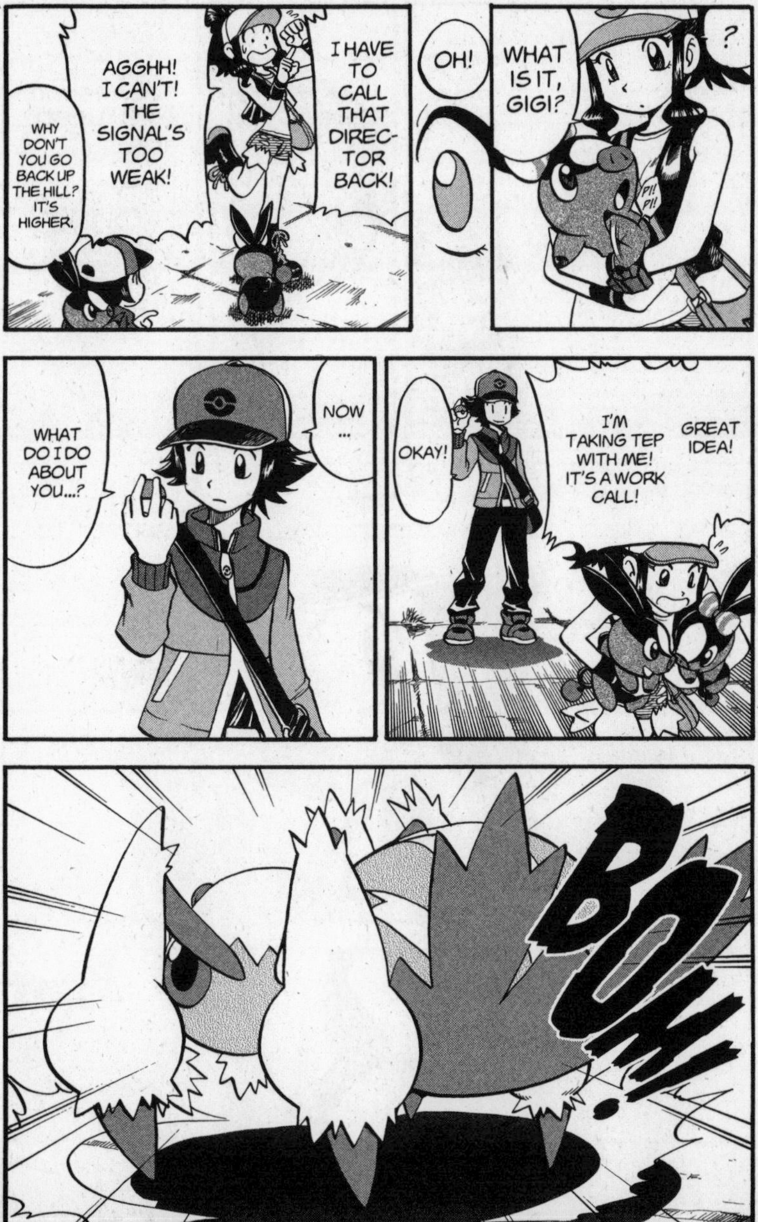
?
WHAT IS IT, GIGI?
OH!
PI! PI!
I HAVE TO CALL THAT DIRECTOR BACK!
AGGHH! I CAN'T! THE SIGNAL'S TOO WEAK!
WHY DON'T YOU GO BACK UP THE HILL? IT'S HIGHER.
GREAT IDEA!
I'M TAKING TEP WITH ME! IT'S A WORK CALL!
OKAY!
NOW ...
WHAT DO I DO ABOUT YOU...?
BOM!

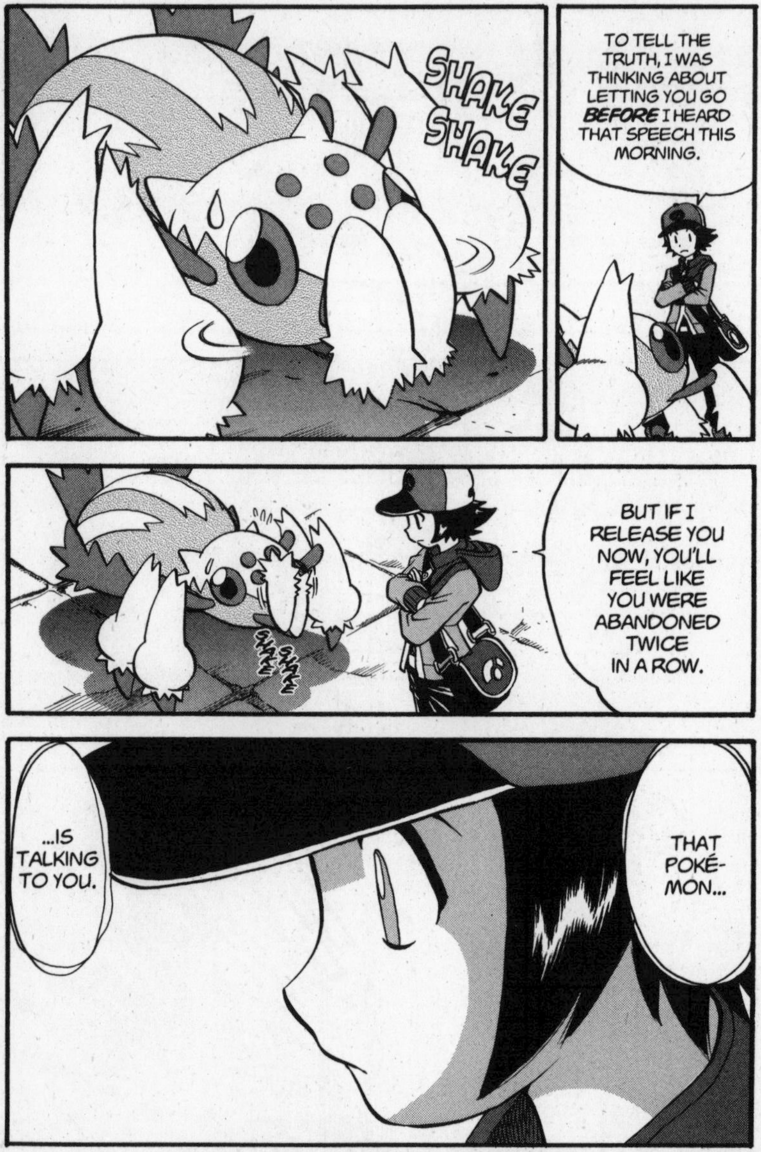
SHAKE SHAKE
TO TELL THE TRUTH, I WAS THINKING ABOUT LETTING YOU GO **BEFORE** I HEARD THAT SPEECH THIS MORNING.
SHAKE SHAKE
BUT IF I RELEASE YOU NOW, YOU'LL FEEL LIKE YOU WERE ABANDONED TWICE IN A ROW.
THAT POKÉ-MON...
...IS TALKING TO YOU.

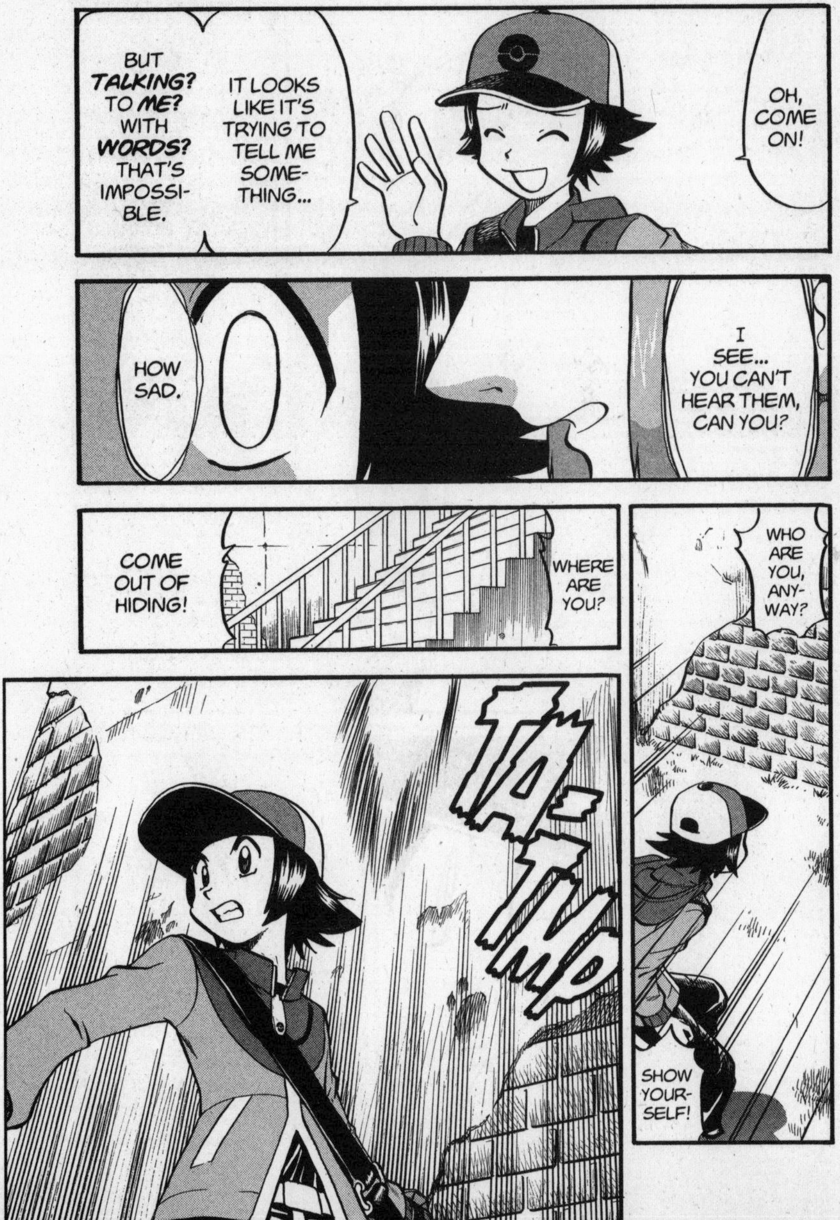
OH, COME ON!
IT LOOKS LIKE IT'S TRYING TO TELL ME SOME-THING...
BUT TALKING? TO ME? WITH WORDS? THAT'S IMPOSSI-BLE.
I SEE... YOU CAN'T HEAR THEM, CAN YOU?
HOW SAD.
WHO ARE YOU, ANY-WAY?
WHERE ARE YOU?
COME OUT OF HIDING!
TA-TMP
SHOW YOUR-SELF!

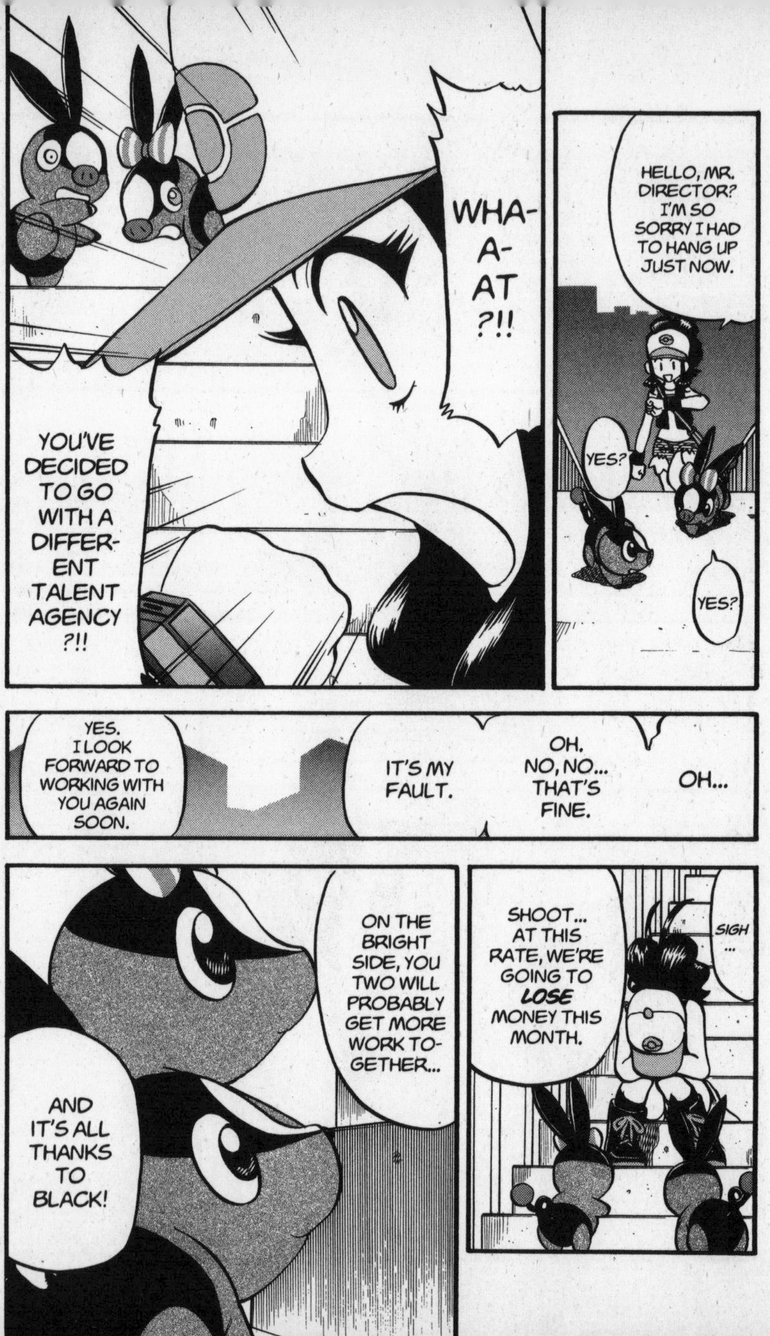
HELLO, MR. DIRECTOR? I'M SO SORRY I HAD TO HANG UP JUST NOW.
YES?
YES?
WHA-A-AT?!!
YOU'VE DECIDED TO GO WITH A DIFFER-ENT TALENT AGENCY?!!
OH...
OH. NO, NO... THAT'S FINE.
IT'S MY FAULT.
YES. I LOOK FORWARD TO WORKING WITH YOU AGAIN SOON.
SIGH...
SHOOT... AT THIS RATE, WE'RE GOING TO *LOSE* MONEY THIS MONTH.
ON THE BRIGHT SIDE, YOU TWO WILL PROBABLY GET MORE WORK TO-GETHER...
AND IT'S ALL THANKS TO BLACK!

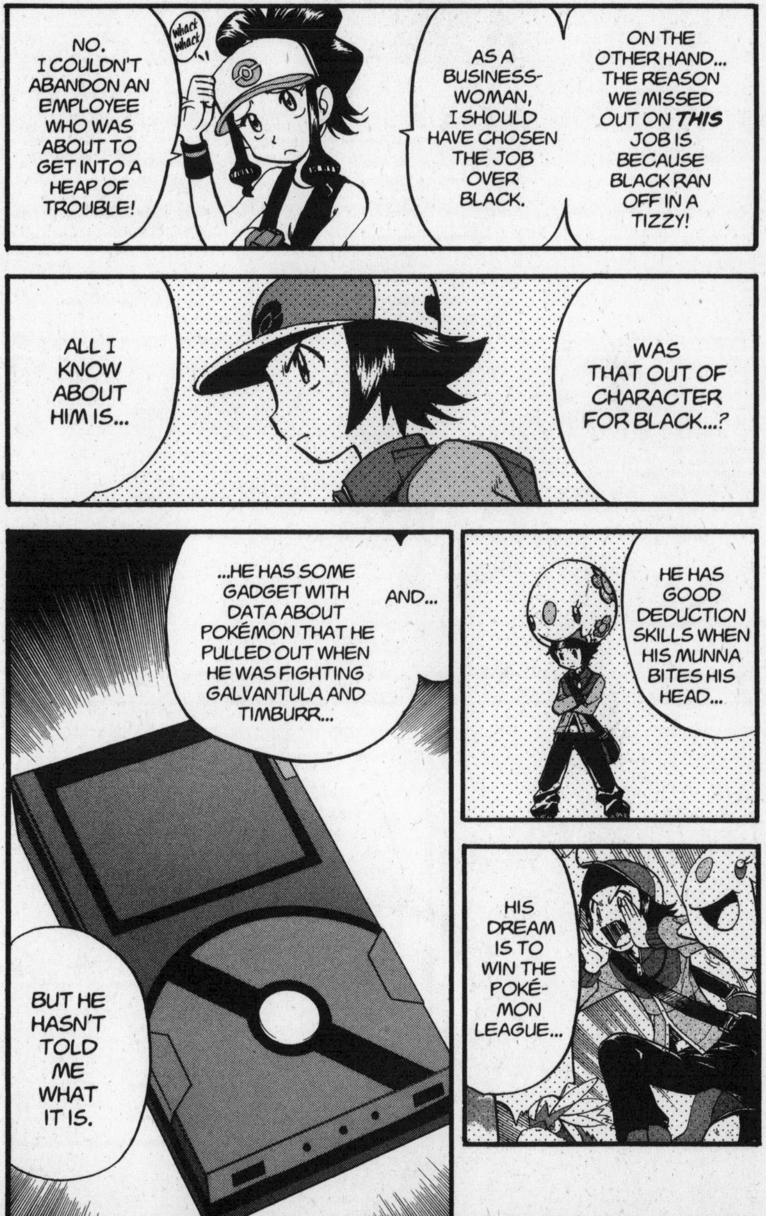
NO. I COULDN'T ABANDON AN EMPLOYEE WHO WAS ABOUT TO GET INTO A HEAP OF TROUBLE!
Whack whack
AS A BUSINESS-WOMAN, I SHOULD HAVE CHOSEN THE JOB OVER BLACK.
ON THE OTHER HAND... THE REASON WE MISSED OUT ON **THIS** JOB IS BECAUSE BLACK RAN OFF IN A TIZZY!
WAS THAT OUT OF CHARACTER FOR BLACK...?
ALL I KNOW ABOUT HIM IS...
HIS DREAM IS TO WIN THE POKÉ-MON LEAGUE...
HE HAS GOOD DEDUCTION SKILLS WHEN HIS MUNNA BITES HIS HEAD...
AND...
...HE HAS SOME GADGET WITH DATA ABOUT POKÉMON THAT HE PULLED OUT WHEN HE WAS FIGHTING GALVANTULA AND TIMBURR...
BUT HE HASN'T TOLD ME WHAT IT IS.

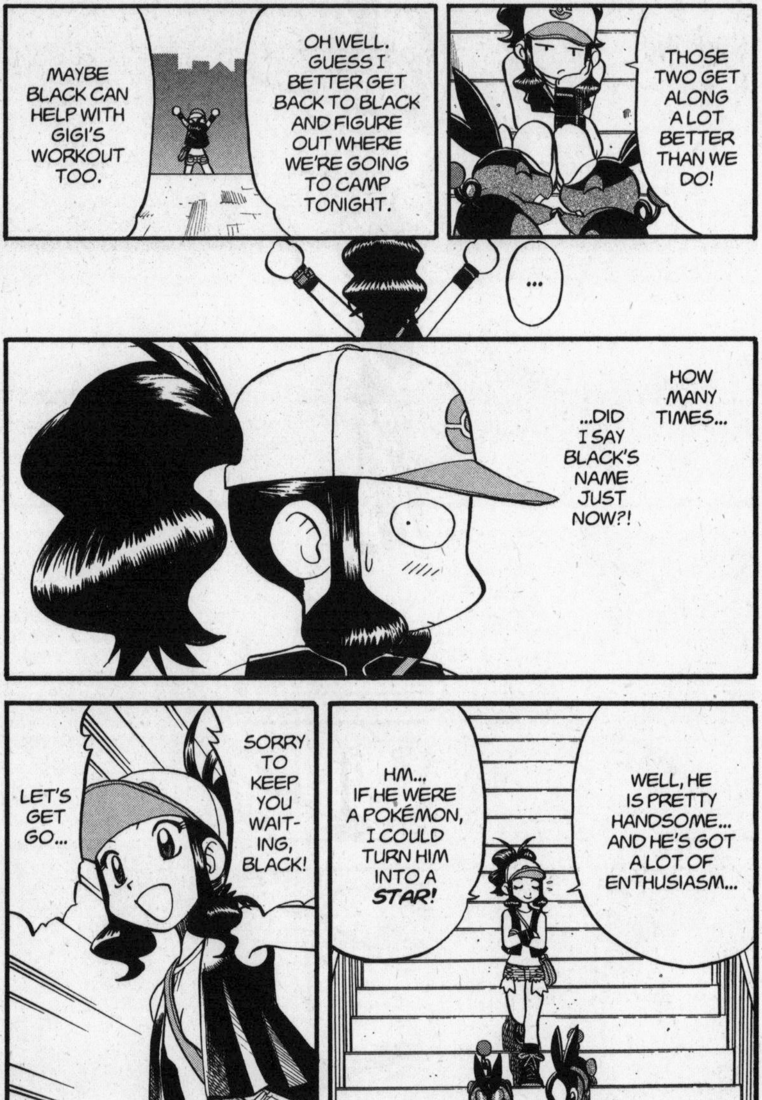
MAYBE BLACK CAN HELP WITH GIGI'S WORKOUT TOO.
OH WELL. GUESS I BETTER GET BACK TO BLACK AND FIGURE OUT WHERE WE'RE GOING TO CAMP TONIGHT.
THOSE TWO GET ALONG A LOT BETTER THAN WE DO!
...
HOW MANY TIMES...
...DID I SAY BLACK'S NAME JUST NOW?!
LET'S GET GO...
SORRY TO KEEP YOU WAIT-ING, BLACK!
HM... IF HE WERE A POKÉMON, I COULD TURN HIM INTO A STAR!
WELL, HE IS PRETTY HANDSOME... AND HE'S GOT A LOT OF ENTHUSIASM...

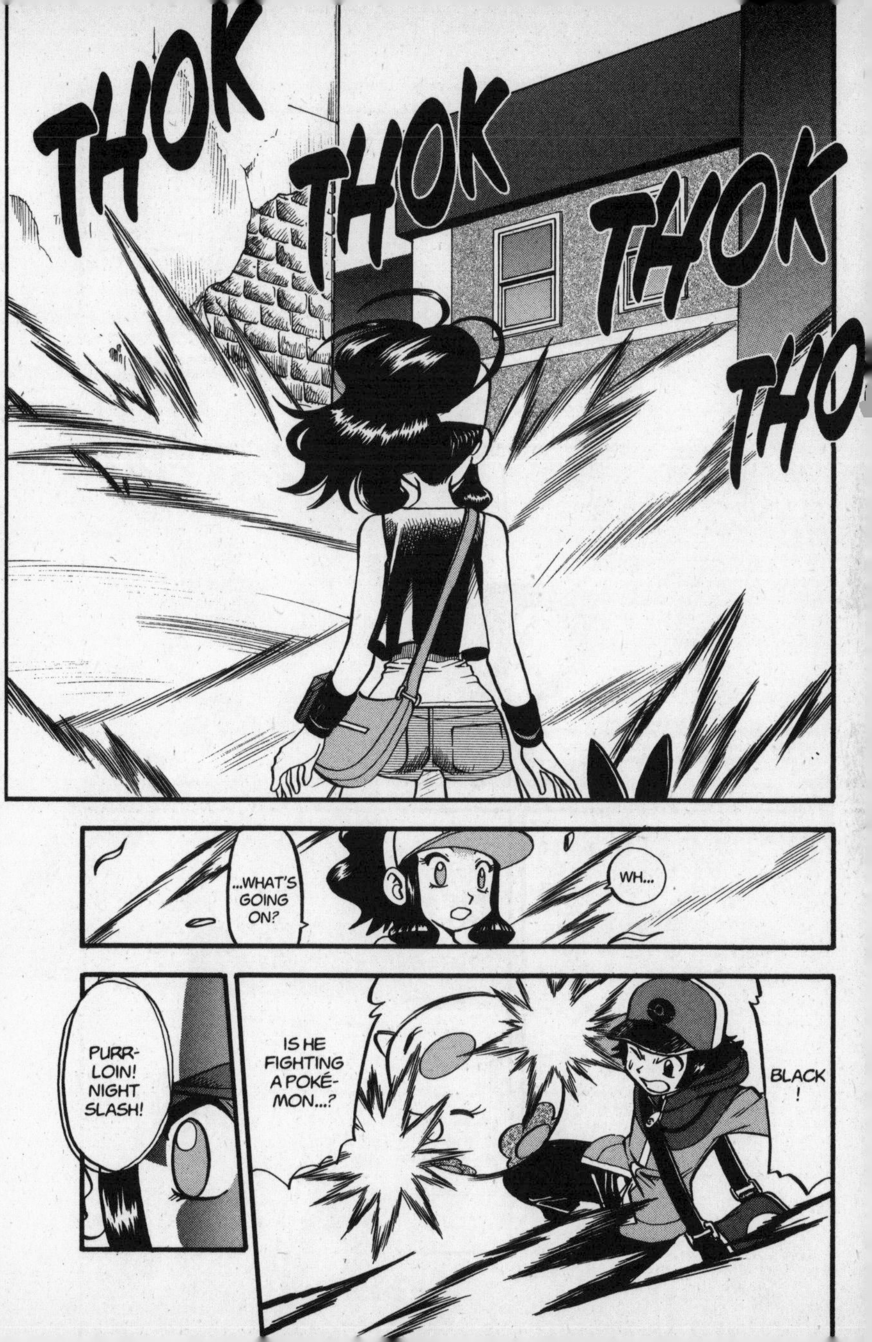
THOK
THOK
THOK
THO
WH...
...WHAT'S GOING ON?
PURR-LOIN! NIGHT SLASH!
IS HE FIGHTING A POKÉMON...?
BLACK!

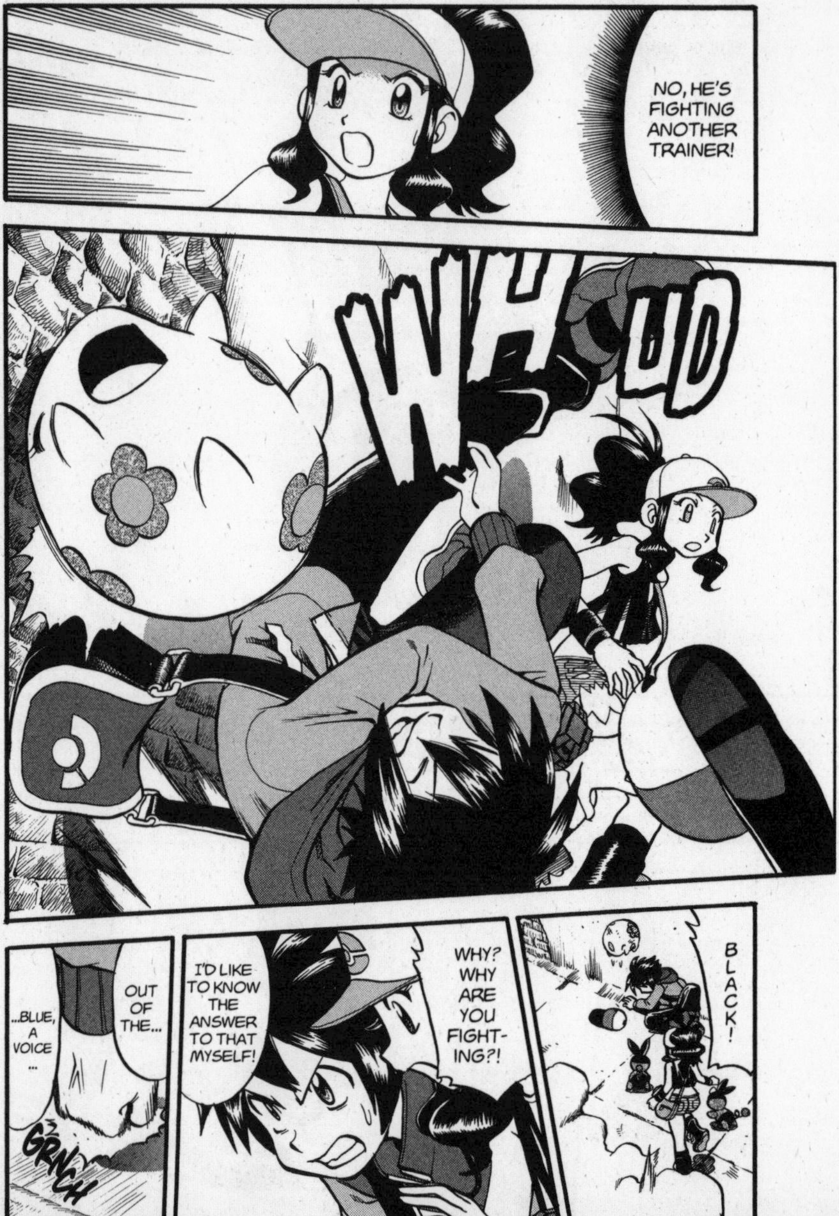
NO, HE'S FIGHTING ANOTHER TRAINER!
WHUD
BLACK!
WHY? WHY ARE YOU FIGHTING?!
I'D LIKE TO KNOW THE ANSWER TO THAT MYSELF!
OUT OF THE...
...BLUE, A VOICE ...
GRNCH

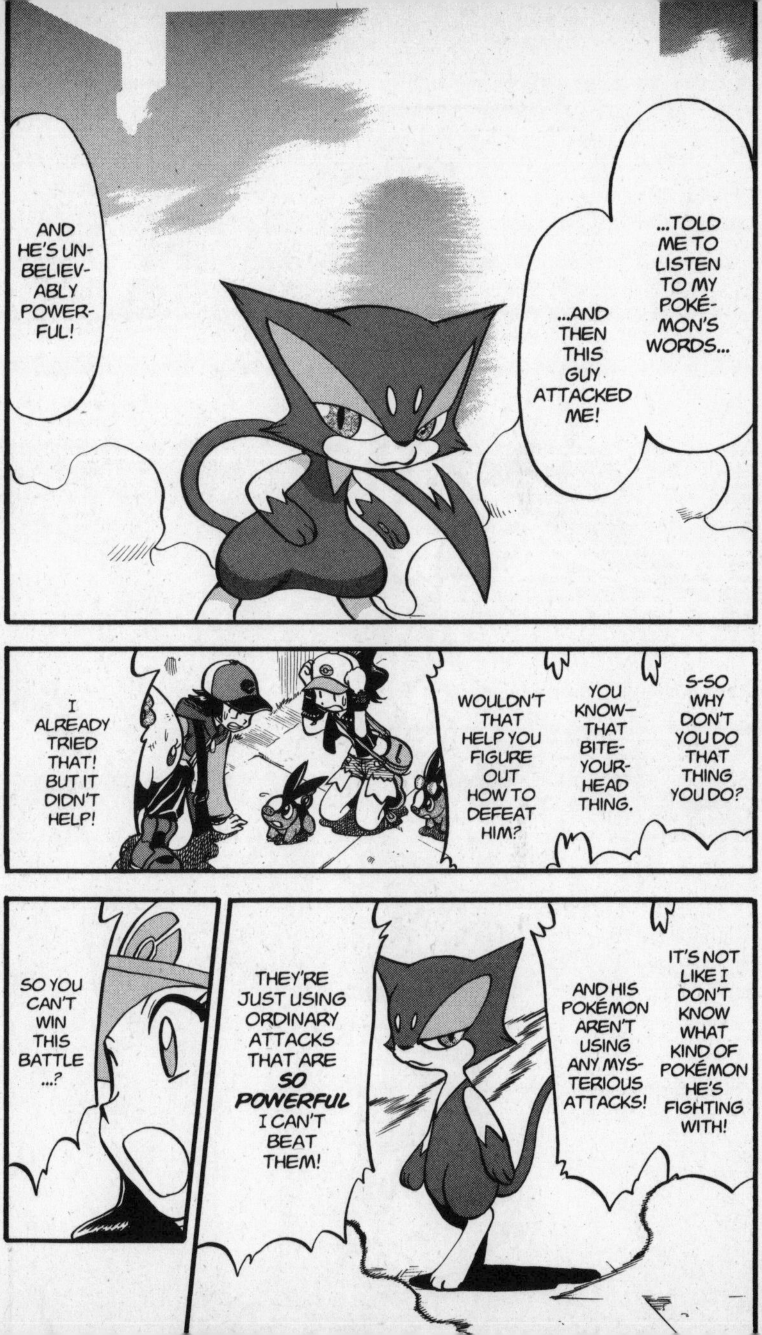

...TOLD ME TO LISTEN TO MY POKÉ-MON'S WORDS...
...AND THEN THIS GUY ATTACKED ME!
AND HE'S UN-BELIEV-ABLY POWER-FUL!
S-SO WHY DON'T YOU DO THAT THING YOU DO?
YOU KNOW—THAT BITE-YOUR-HEAD THING.
WOULDN'T THAT HELP YOU FIGURE OUT HOW TO DEFEAT HIM?
I ALREADY TRIED THAT! BUT IT DIDN'T HELP!
IT'S NOT LIKE I DON'T KNOW WHAT KIND OF POKÉMON HE'S FIGHTING WITH!
AND HIS POKÉMON AREN'T USING ANY MYS-TERIOUS ATTACKS!
THEY'RE JUST USING ORDINARY ATTACKS THAT ARE **SO POWERFUL** I CAN'T BEAT THEM!
SO YOU CAN'T WIN THIS BATTLE ...?

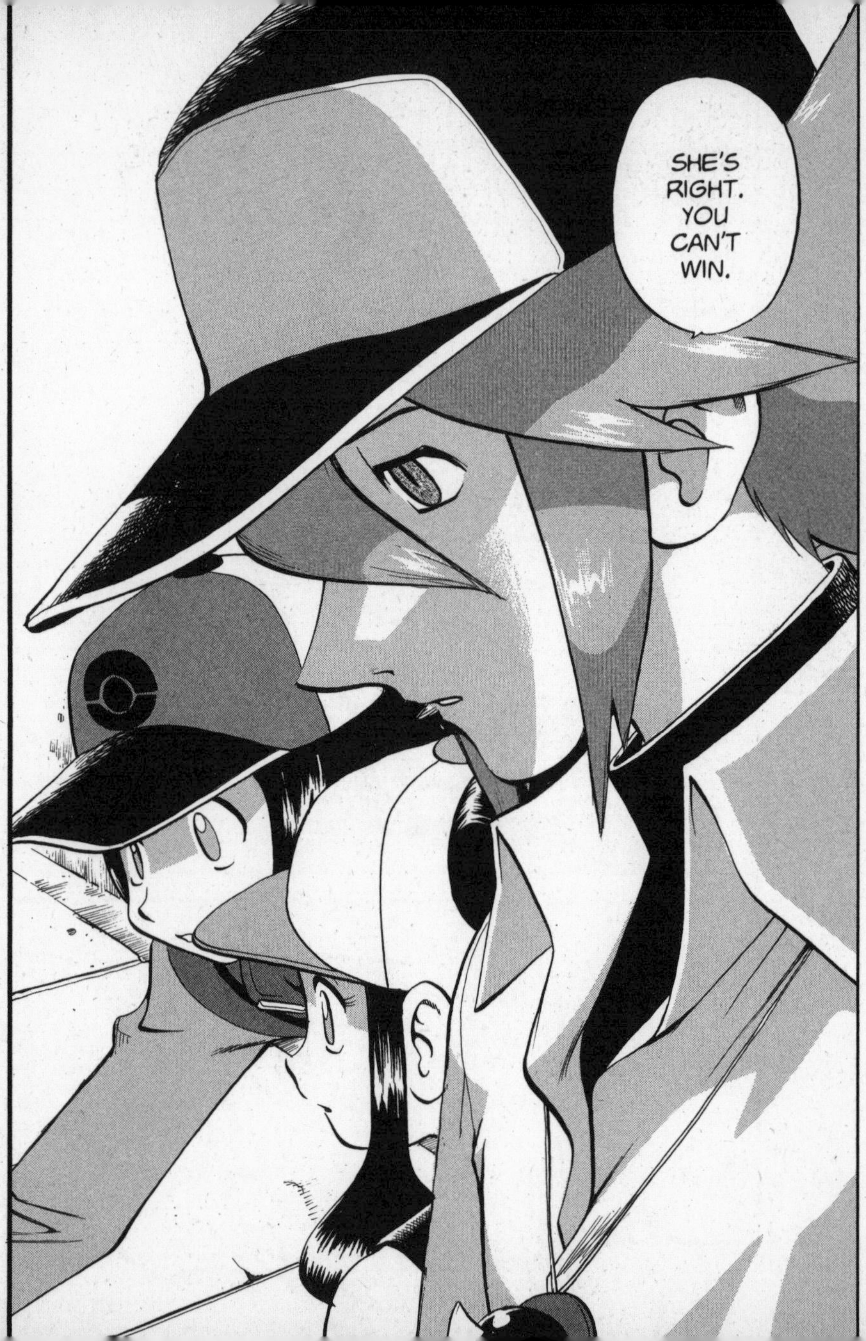
SHE'S RIGHT. YOU CAN'T WIN.

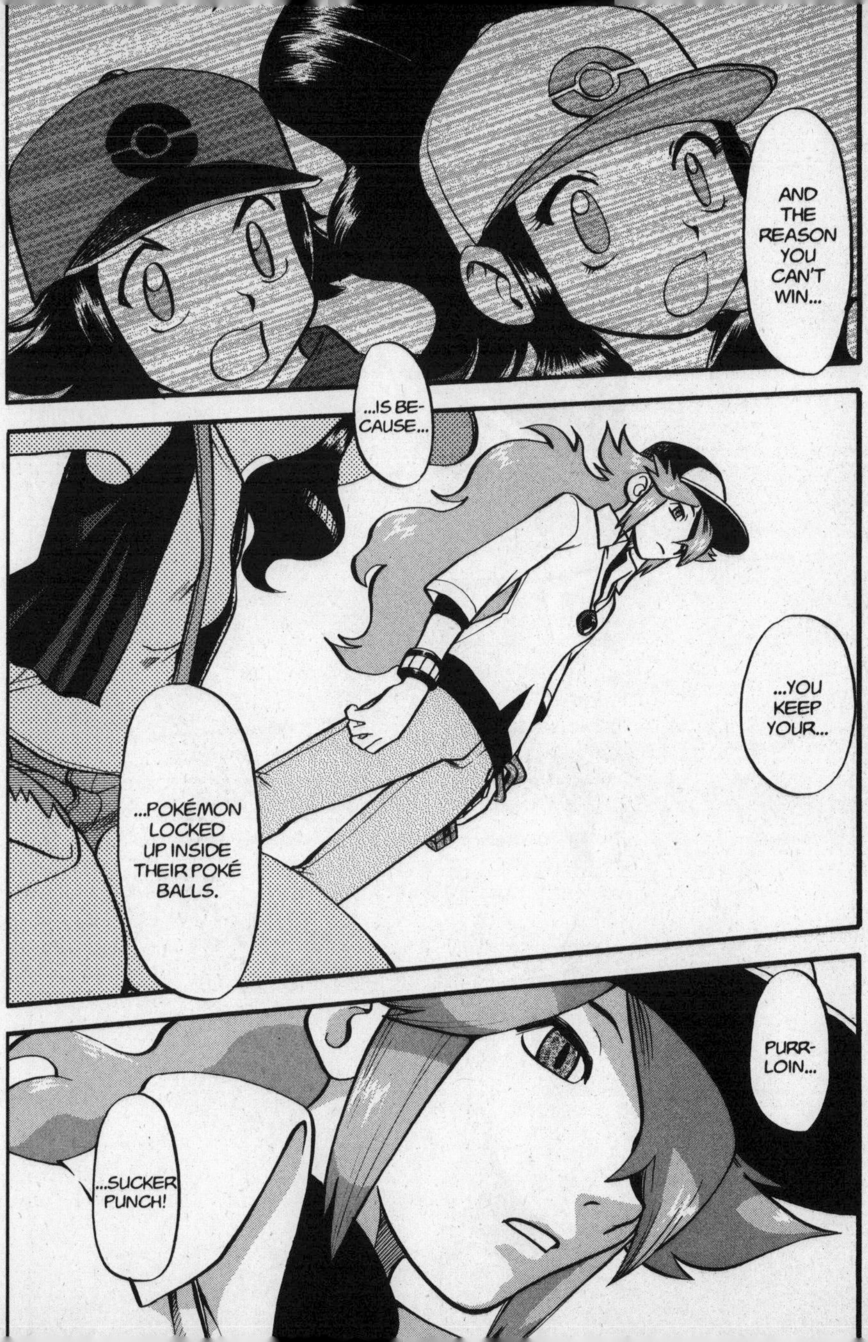
AND THE REASON YOU CAN'T WIN...
...IS BE-CAUSE...
...YOU KEEP YOUR...
...POKÉMON LOCKED UP INSIDE THEIR POKÉ BALLS.
PURR-LOIN...
...SUCKER PUNCH!

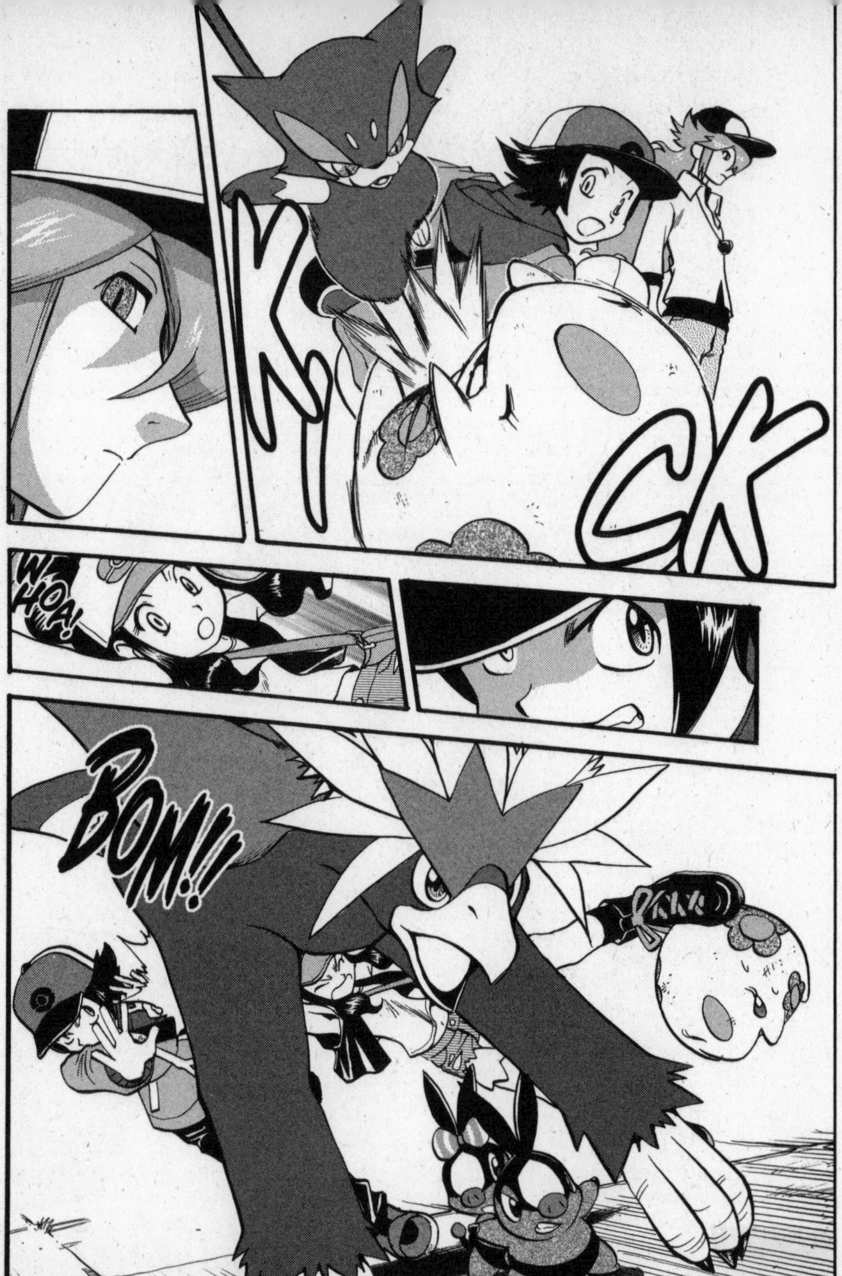
KICK
WHOA!
BOM!!

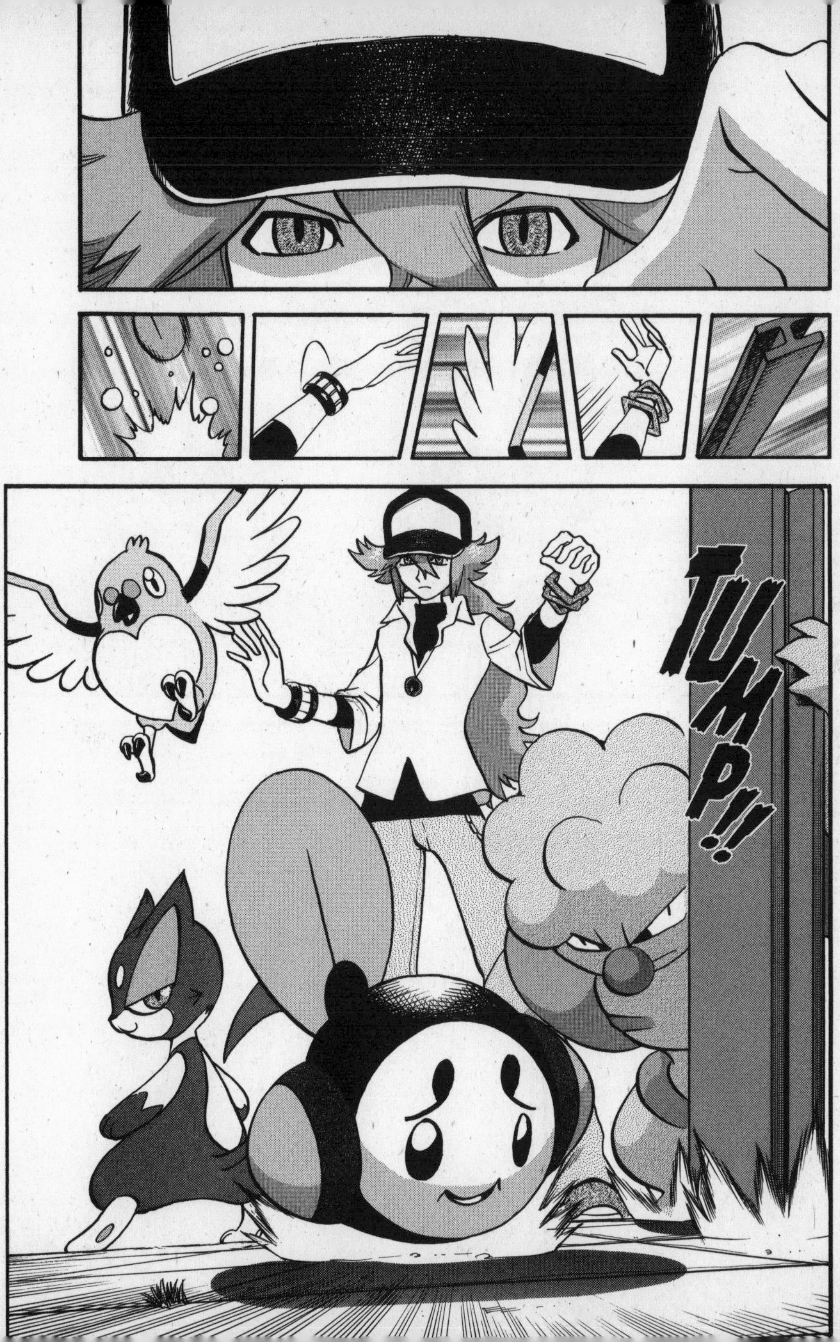
TUMP!!

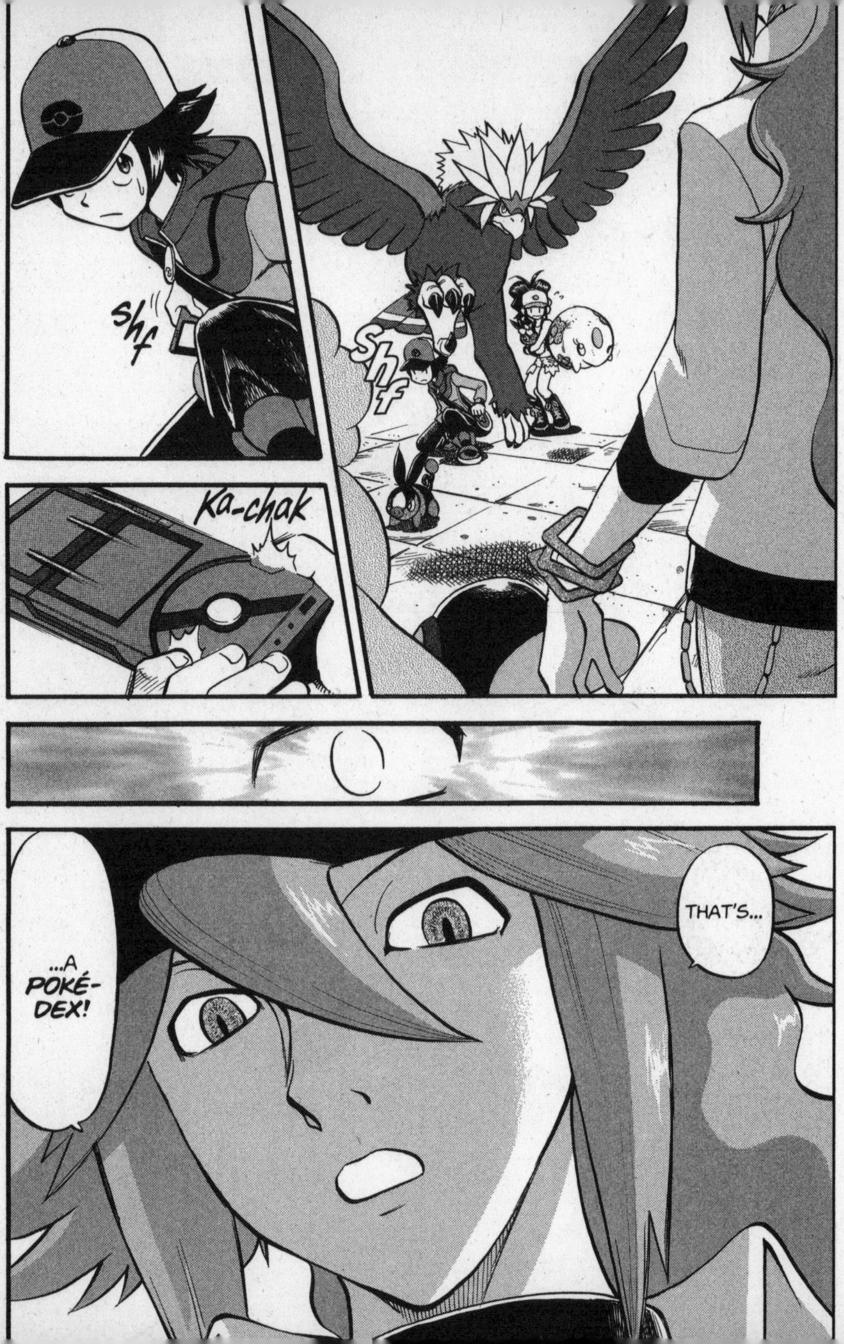

SHF
SHF
KA-CHAK
THAT'S...
...A POKÉ-DEX!

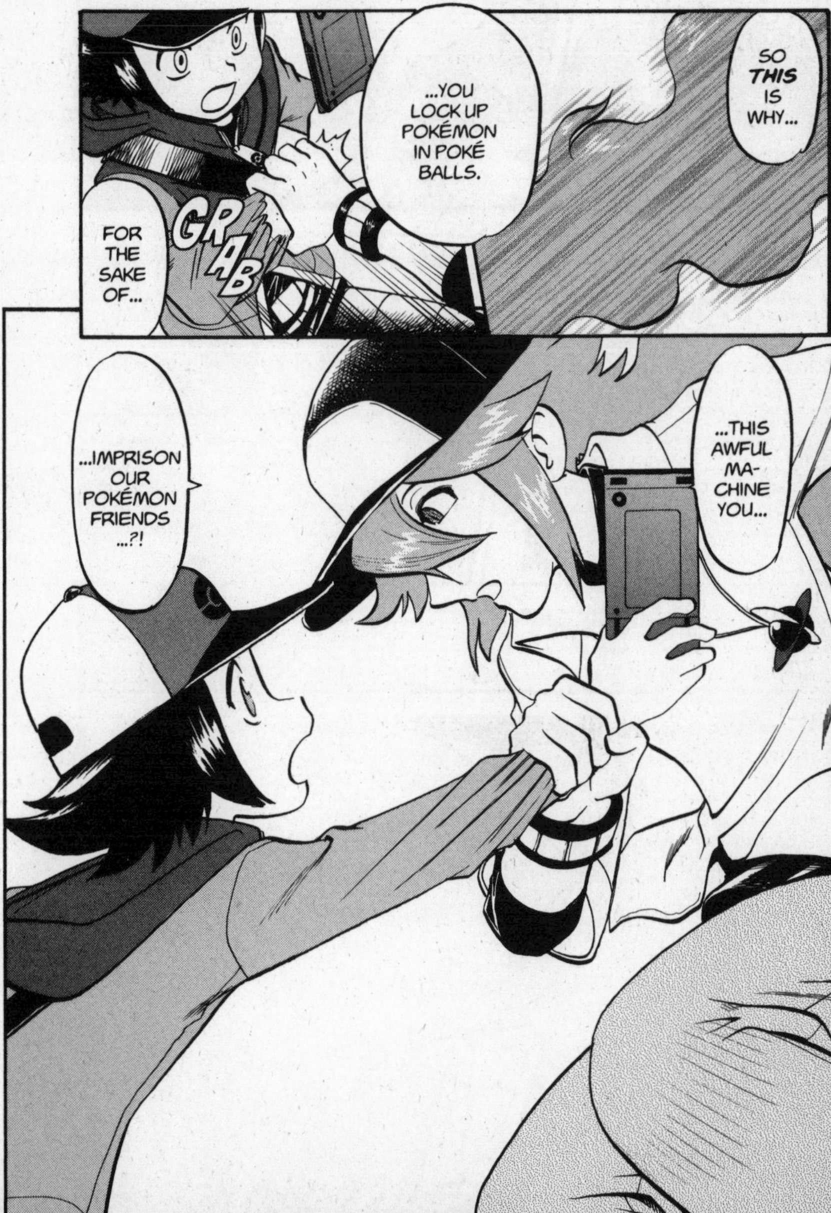
SO THIS IS WHY...
...YOU LOCK UP POKÉMON IN POKÉ BALLS.
GRAB
FOR THE SAKE OF...
...THIS AWFUL MA-CHINE YOU...
...IMPRISON OUR POKÉMON FRIENDS ...?!

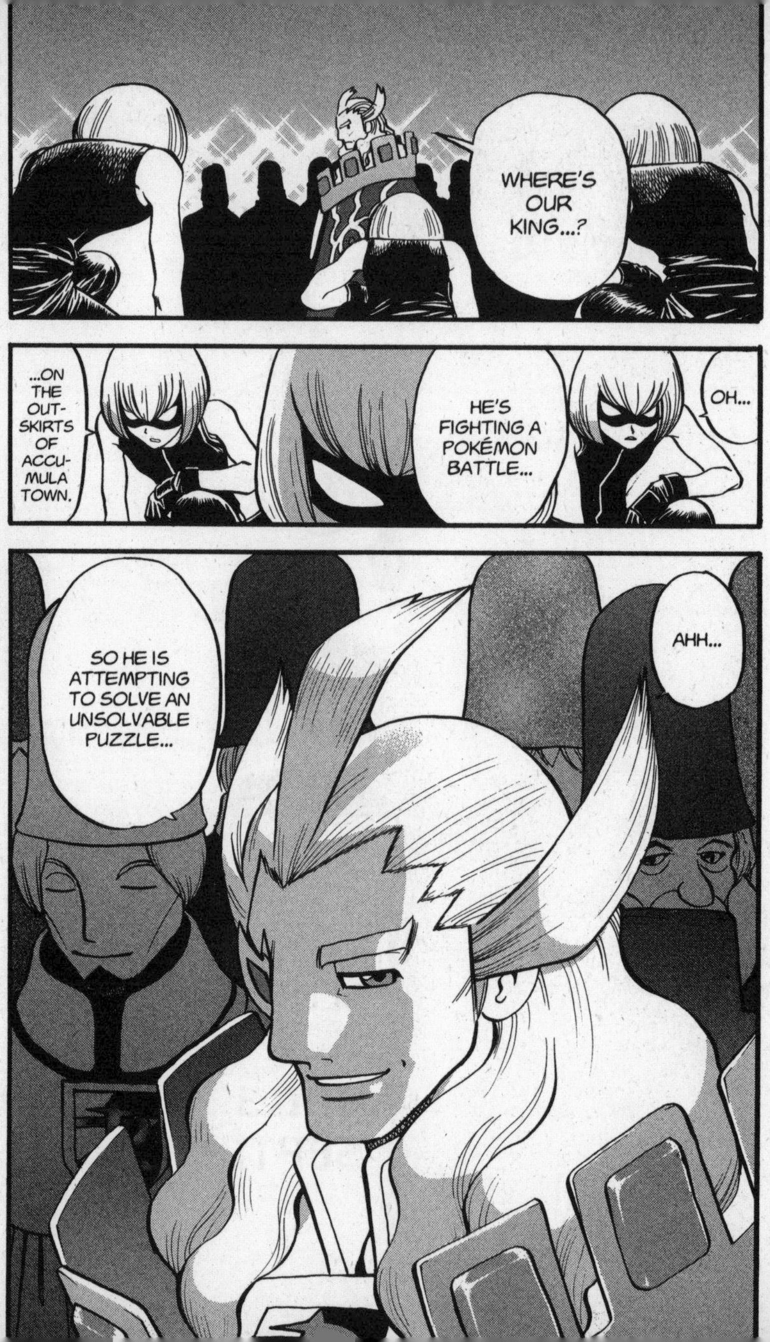
WHERE'S OUR KING...?
OH...
HE'S FIGHTING A POKÉMON BATTLE...
...ON THE OUT-SKIRTS OF ACCU-MULA TOWN.
AHH...
SO HE IS ATTEMPTING TO SOLVE AN UNSOLVABLE PUZZLE...

# More Adventures COMING SOON...

Team Plasma member N has the nerve to tell Black he isn't in touch with his Pokémon's feelings. Them's fighting words—literally! Which of the two trainers has the best relationship with his Pokémon, and will that help him win a heated Pokémon Battle...?

**HEY! WHY WON'T WHITE HELP BLACK FIGHT...?**

**VOL.3 AVAILABLE SEPTEMBER 2011!**

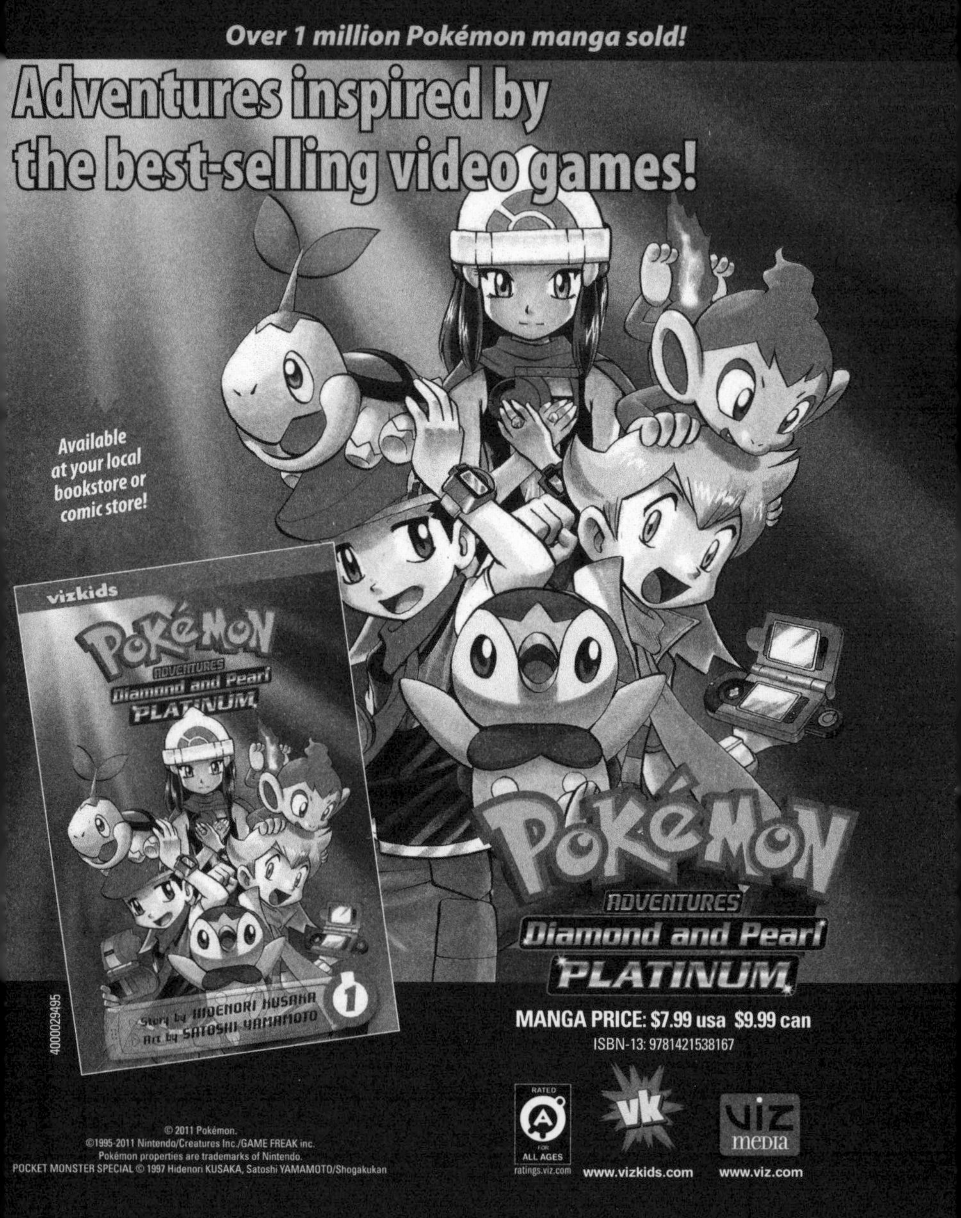
Over 1 million Pokémon manga sold!
Adventures inspired by the best-selling video games!
Available at your local bookstore or comic store!
vizkids
POKÉMON ADVENTURES Diamond and Pearl PLATINUM
Story by HIDENORI KUSAKA
Art by SATOSHI YAMAMOTO
1
4000029495
POKÉMON
ADVENTURES
Diamond and Pearl
PLATINUM
MANGA PRICE: $7.99 usa $9.99 can
ISBN-13: 9781421538167
RATED A FOR ALL AGES
ratings.viz.com
vk
www.vizkids.com
VIZ media
www.viz.com
© 2011 Pokémon.
©1995-2011 Nintendo/Creatures Inc./GAME FREAK inc.
Pokémon properties are trademarks of Nintendo.
POCKET MONSTER SPECIAL © 1997 Hidenori KUSAKA, Satoshi YAMAMOTO/Shogakukan

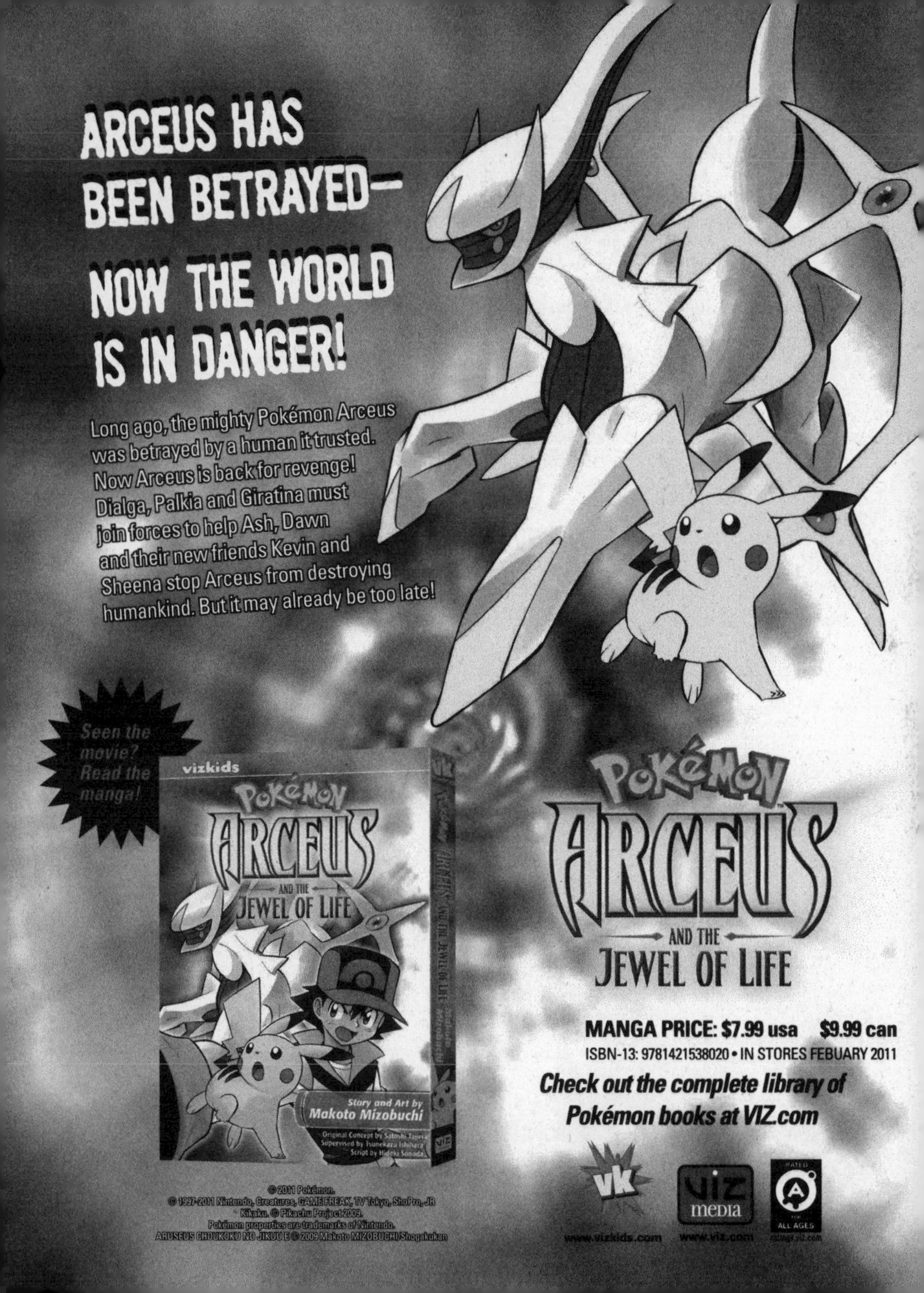
ARCEUS HAS BEEN BETRAYED—
NOW THE WORLD IS IN DANGER!
Long ago, the mighty Pokémon Arceus was betrayed by a human it trusted. Now Arceus is back for revenge! Dialga, Palkia and Giratina must join forces to help Ash, Dawn and their new friends Kevin and Sheena stop Arceus from destroying humankind. But it may already be too late!
Seen the movie? Read the manga!
vizkids
POKÉMON ARCEUS AND THE JEWEL OF LIFE
Story and Art by Makoto Mizobuchi
Original Concept by Satoshi Tajiri
Supervised by Tsunekazu Ishihara
Script by Hideki Sonoda
POKÉMON
ARCEUS
AND THE
JEWEL OF LIFE
MANGA PRICE: $7.99 usa $9.99 can
ISBN-13: 9781421538020 • IN STORES FEBUARY 2011
Check out the complete library of Pokémon books at VIZ.com
© 2011 Pokémon.
© 1997-2011 Nintendo, Creatures, GAME FREAK, TV Tokyo, ShoPro, JR Kikaku. © Pikachu Project 2009.
Pokémon properties are trademarks of Nintendo.
ARUSEUS CHOUKOKU NO JIKUU E © 2009 Makoto MIZOBUCHI/Shogakukan
vk
VIZ media
RATED A ALL AGES
www.vizkids.com
www.viz.com
ratings.viz.com